MW01165907

Dreams of a Freezing Ocean

Volume 1

S.G. Kubrak

ISBN: 978-1-7375922-0-4

DEDICATION

This anthology would never have seen the light of day without the tireless support of some very important people. My wife Allie, whose understanding of this incessant need for me to write has only grown stronger over the years. My daughter Talia, an author in her own right, and the inspiration of many of my stories. My mother Kathleen, also a writer, who set me on this path many decades ago. Finally, to my teachers and professors over the years who cultivated a drive to embrace my creative side and be brave enough to let the world share.

I am forever in their debt.

ACKNOWLEDGMENTS

I gratefully acknowledge the following people
for their contributions and inspiration

Editor/Proofreader
Monica Neumark

Cover design
Allie Shaw

Cover photo
SG Kubrak, 12/26/2020, Broadway Beach, Cape May, New Jersey

Inspiration for "The Qutquisition of Reston"
"Solarpunk: Post-Industrial Design and Aesthetics" by Eric Hunting
https://medium.com/@erichunting/solarpunk-post-industrial-design-
and-aesthetics-1ecb350c28b6

Table of Contents

Inquefish

I watched the sea from the beach, waiting. The purple-black waves crashed on the shore with a loud but comforting crash. The full moon shone overhead in a cloudless inky black star-filled sky.

Beyond the breakers, the featureless ocean stretched to the horizon, partially hidden in grey haze.

I passed the time while I sat by watching horseshoe crabs emerge from the waves. They were venturing to the beach to lay their eggs and then return to the sea. They were so primitive, and yet perfect, not evolving in millions of years.

The beach was filled with the noises of nocturnal life. A mockingbird called in the stand of pine trees which lay behind the beach. The local pack of dogs barked in the distance. There were dolphins feeding beyond the breakers, and occasionally I could hear a splash as one of them breached.

I sat there on the beach as I had almost every summer night since my childhood. I buried my feet in the cool sand and my hands in the pockets of my sweatshirt. Autumn drew near, and I would soon have to leave my family's summer beach house and head to the university.

But going to college to begin my undergraduate degree in marine biology did not hold the same excitement as this particular night. Both had me nervous and excited, but this was real-life fieldwork, I told myself, not sitting in a lab dissecting fetal pigs. I hoped tonight would be the first night I would see them.

The school moved up slowly from the equator where they had been spotted. At first, they meandered in the doldrums. For a year they drifted listlessly in that warm, breezeless stretch of ocean. Then, last spring, they caught the Gulf Stream and had been riding up the coast ever since.

Sometimes they would get off the great river in the ocean, staying within sight of the coast for weeks, always heading north. They would sit offshore during the nights, the lights from their eyes glinting in the distance like fireflies blown out to sea. As if they were watching us.

No one knew where they came from. There were theories they were a newly discovered species of flying fish or eel. Others believed they might have been native to an undersea thermal vent, and some catastrophe brought them to the surface. Still, there were others, myself included, who thought their appearance directly connected to an unexpected meteor shower over Ascension Island last year.

Research vessels had been dispatched to study our new visitors. They were captured and dissected with relative ease, offering no resistance.

They were deemed primitive and harmless possessing simple organs and no offensive capabilities. The single eye perched on the solitary eyestalk glowed with a form of bioluminescence, like the anglerfish. But these eyes glowed blue-white with the brilliance of a spotlight. Biologists believed they were powered like electric eels, electrolytes that ran the length of what could best be described as their spines. They had no blood, but circulated nourishment through a black, ink-like fluid that filled all the cavities in their bodies - another common ability amongst marine animals - similar to sponges and shellfish.

Compelling yet disturbing, these aspects were almost impossible for any organism: They did not eat or breathe. With no obvious organs or appendages for movement, they appeared to float like small, noiseless hovercraft. Theories abounded as to the mechanism; lift from thermal currents, optical illusion, and magnetic levitation. All were plausible but none were proven.

These characteristics were so remarkable consternated scientists became obsessed with them. The visitors were dubbed the "biological find of the century."

I *had* to see these creatures. At four in the morning, the other spectators gave up on seeing them. These visitors would not come close to shore with any reliability, and tonight appeared to be another disappointment. I stayed hoping for a glimpse.

I didn't have to wait much longer for the visitors to arrive. Out on the horizon, I saw a light - white, small and distant. At first, I thought it might be a ship, but after a few minutes, I counted upwards of sixty lights. If they were ships it would be a small armada.

There they were, "Inquefish" as they were beginning to be called, and I was the first person in New Jersey to see them.

The inquefish were congregating beyond the breakers. If they were dolphins I would assume they were feeding, but apparently, inquefish did not feed. I could not make out their shapes; only the lights were visible. I read their bodies were jet black, again like black ink. They must have been blending in with the water so well they were camouflaged.

After a few minutes, I assumed the inquefish were resting for the evening and would head back out to sea when dawn came. I was wrong.

I saw a light ride up the backside of a wave, effortlessly. The wave crested and broke, and the light slid onto the shore. Quickly I got up from my seat on a piece of driftwood and walked toward the beach, trying to get a better view.

I could see the inquefish, floating mere inches over the sand. Roughly the size of a German shepherd, its body had an ovoid shape, with a flat bottom. On the front side, it sported the single eyestalk, almost two feet long. Perched atop the eyestalk sat the eye, the size of a teacup saucer. It glowed with an icy brilliance that swept across the shore like a searchlight. Its black body, featureless and smooth, barely reflected any light, almost as if it weren't there at all.

It scanned the shoreline, like a soldier checking a beachhead. I never heard of anyone interacting with them on the land before and had no intention of being the first. It scanned the area with stoic indifference, floating above the sand, but making no impression on the surface.

Suddenly it turned back toward the breakers and to its companions waiting offshore. Its light dimmed and brightened in a pattern for a few moments and then stopped flashing, returning to its constant brilliance. The pattern was then repeated by several of its companions outside the breakers. Then another light crested a wave, and then another, and still another.

Fear overtook me, and I scrambled from the shore as fast as I could, heading back to my piece of driftwood. Soon the beach held as many as thirty inquefish scouring the shoreline with their lights making absolutely no noise. An Inquefish spotted the group of horseshoe crabs and quickly glided over to them. It stopped mere inches from one of them. In an instant the inquefish pressed its eye against the horseshoe crab, the giant orb flashing repeatedly. The crab jumped, but then fell motionless. My breath quickened and my hands shook as adrenaline coursed through my body. Over the pounding of furiously pumping heart, I looked around in shock; several of the other inquefish were doing the same, attacking crabs one by one. Others were moving up the beach, towards me.

Still hidden in the darkness, I searched around the beach for a safe place to hide and yet still watch. The closest place was a lifeguard tower. It's seat, at least seven feet above the sand, would make a safe perch. I climbed to the top and hoped it would be out of the inquefish's reach.

Peering down from my perch, I panted hard, and my heart raced. Five inquefish gathered around the base of my wooden tower, scanning its surface with their lights. The lights made their way up the tower and then found me. They raced over every part of my body, varying in intensity. I knew they floated, and I prayed they could not fly.

They circled the tower like deadly silent sharks, casting their lights. After a time, one of them pressed its eye against a leg of the tower and started flashing. I could smell wood burning and hoped the tower would not suddenly catch fire. Another turned straight up at me flashing madly. I could smell ozone in the air, and the hairs burned on my legs, I pulled my feet up quickly and stood on the seat. Their range was limited after all.

In fear, I scanned around the tower for something to defend myself, only to find nothing available. Out of desperation, I ripped a loose board from the back of the chair and swung it at the nearest inquefish. It quickly turned and flashed at the board with an unearthly intensity, splintering the wood and temporarily blinding me. My arm seared with pain and I smelled my flesh burning. I jerked myself back into the chair and held tightly, eyes squeezed shut, waiting to be burned alive. After a moment I opened my eyes. The board practically exploded in my hands; all that was left was the bit I grasped. My arm was burned and blistered up to the elbow, and my sweatshirt burned away to my shoulder. No one ever thought of them to be aggressive, or that their lights provided anything other than illumination. We were wrong.

Something changed, and the inquefish adopted a more menacing, unforeseen aspect. Like salmon which become enormous and aggressive before they run upstream.

After a while, they gave up on me and scoured the beach again. I could not understand why they had not finished me off or destroyed the tower beneath me. Then I realized it acted in self-defense. It eliminated the board, the immediate threat, and then moved onto easier prey. That defensive reaction must have used enormous energy.

Out of the corner of my eye, I saw something grey streak by. A rabbit ran across the beach as fast as it could toward the stand of trees. An inquefish closely followed it, making no sound and moving with alarming speed. When it was within a foot of the rabbit, it flashed its light at it. In an agonizingly slow moment, the rabbit screamed, then tumbled to a stop in the sand. The inquefish descended upon its prey and pressed its eye to the rabbit's frantically twitching body. I expected the inquefish to flash again, but instead, the light went out. Cradling my arm, I leaned forward over the back of the tower and tried to get a better view. I hoped the structure would not topple beneath me. How was a scared rabbit a threat to them? Why did they give up on me?

Around the circumference of its solitary eye, black fluid poured from the inquefish. Horrified, I wondered if this was how they fed, digesting their prey from the outside like a housefly with a stolen morsel. After a moment, the body of the motionless rabbit was covered in the inky tar-like fluid, and the inquefish lost interest. It moved away and began scanning the beach again.

A flash of light from the stand of trees and I could hear the pack of dogs barking and growling. One by one, the barks stopped with a whine, associated with a flash of electric light. The dogs were suffering the fate I narrowly avoided.

The air filled with the putrid smell of burning flesh and hair. The inquefish scoured every inch of it searching for other prey. Their range was limited to a few feet from the ground, but nothing survived below that.

I checked the dead rabbit; the tar slowly bubbled, barely noticeable at first, but there was motion.

After several minutes, lights appeared at the entrance to the stand of trees as the inquefish came back down towards the shore. One by one the inquefish swam back out into the sea. They effortlessly climbed the face of the breakers and joined the others waiting just offshore. I had no idea why they had gone on this orgy of killing for no apparent reason. About to jump off the guard tower, I took one last glance at the rabbit.

The tar formed definite bubbles on the surface of the dead animal. The carcass was smaller, and I noticed little lights begin to flash from the surface of the tar. At first, they were motionless but then began to move around. Eventually, tiny eyestalks protruded from the bubbles. The rabbit soon appeared as if it had swallowed a light bulb and light escaped from its pores. Then it all made sense.

The inquefish came ashore to spawn.

The rabbit was covered in twenty or so baby inquefish, all about the size of my palm. The little ones frolicked over the body, engaging in wrestling matches with each other, and others flashed the carcass. The smell of burning flesh nearly overpowered me.

Amazingly, as I watched, the inquefish grew larger as the carcass grew smaller. They did not appear to be eating it but were digesting the body nonetheless. Electric arcs jumped around the body, and with each flash, the spawn grew more energized.

Within minutes the baby visitors doubled in size and were wandering around the remains of the rabbit. They scoured the beach like their parents, burning the grass and flashing at anything that moved.

The first light of dawn began to break over the haze at the horizon; the sky took on a sickly pink-grey hue. The rabbit skeleton, bleached and crushed, barely noticeable amid the white sand and the tufts of burnt beach grass.

In unison, the babies turned toward the sea and began making tentative moves toward the shore. From the stand of trees, dozens of babies headed towards the breakers. My mind numbed at the pernicious fecundity of the inquefish.

The new inquefish reached the shore and were climbing the waves as nimbly as their parents did. They joined the others who danced and flashed in celebration of the new members of their school.

The inquefish doubled in number. At times, the line of the sea outside the breakers filled with glowing eyes, darting back and forth over the water, utterly noiseless. The entire beach stretched out devoid of animal life. The birds fled. The wind had not yet shifted from the land to the shore. All I could hear was the low roar of the waves, and the blood pounding in my ears.

The dawn light encouraged me to come down from my perch. I jumped to the cold sand, holding my burned arm close to my body, and examined the burned spot on the leg of the tower. It was burned almost all the way through and I was fortunate that I didn't break and send me tumbling to the sand, to my demise.

The inquefish were drifting further out to sea, with the little ones in the rear. If there were any predictability left to these creatures, they would be headed north again.

I stood there for a moment, staring at the blue-white lights drifting off to the horizon. I knew, from the research, this must have been the first stop they made. I also knew the shore and the currents so well in this area that I always felt at home here. Now that feeling had been violated, my pleasant memories were raped. This beach would never be the same again.

A chill shot up the length of my spine and my heart fluttered as fear ripped through my body. I *did* know these waters well, and how long it took something to swim out to sea and then northward. I turned and ran from the beach as fast as I could. I had to tell somebody, anybody who would listen. People had to be warned. More importantly, I had to tell my family. At the rate they moved, by tonight, the inquefish would be at the worst place possible to come ashore.

New York City.

Home.

The Rogue

Overhead, the disk of the Milky Way hangs like a bucket of paint splattered across a black canvas. This glowing backdrop provides the only natural light, illuminating the surface of the world. Darker than moonlight, this is the brightest of days on this quickly rotating planet. Every seven hours this side rotates in and out of view of the galaxy. Every seven hours it is plunged into impenetrable inky darkness. The individual halo star-clusters of the galaxy are visible then, mere pinpricks in the curtain of the endless night.

Toward the core of the galaxy, the nursery system of this world teems with life, basking in the glow of two yellow stars. Where this world was is now an empty orbit, a hole in the family portrait riven by the gravity of two gas giants that had their way with their smaller siblings.

On the third 'day' the two large moons of this world parade across the backdrop of the galaxy. Visible by virtue of their invisibility, the circular silhouettes stroll through their neighborhood, providing a tantalizing reminder this world is not completely alone. A miniature family in nocturne, pirouetting and pulling on each other.

Moving down through the thick, yet transparent atmosphere, a purple and orange hue hugs the land. The air buzzes with the sounds of insects taking advantage of the full illumination. Blue-white lights reflect off the nearly featureless landscape. A thick purple carpet stretches out to the horizon in all directions, concentrating in hallows, and thinning out on peaks. Insects skitter over this carpet, both living in and feeding upon, it's biomass. This carpet of chimeric fungi is the dominant form of life on this planet, digesting rock through chemosynthesis and incorporating it into its structure.

Much of the land surface is basalt rock, driven to the surface by tidal heating from the dance of the three bodies. Lava bubbles here and there and the hydrogen sulfide is greedily absorbed by fungal stalks rising from the carpet.

Deep in the singular equatorial ocean, animal forms of life live on yet more hydrogen sulfide expelled from hydrothermal vents.

Enveloped in absolute darkness, even starlight is a thing of fantasy. The fungi do not enter the aquatic environment, for it is much too acidic.

At the confluence between the land and water, the bioluminescent insects scatter, driven forward by an unseen form. After a moment they settle, hugging the slowly lapping water, their panicked chirping replaced by mating calls.

With barely a respite, the insects scatter again, raising alarm. A rock skips across the shore. A bright white light turns on, illuminating a helmeted human face.

Are You Sure She Is Who You Think She Is?

Click

She smiled as the tumbler fell on the lock and paused her hands for just a second longer. With a hint of trepidation, she waited for the extra lock to click into place, but she knew there wouldn't be one. The secondary lock was the easiest to disable and the first to go. With a flick of her wrist, she spun open the combination lock and clicked open the handle.

The stack of bills in the center of the safe caught her eye and she reached in and picked them up. Taking them out, she put them on the floor in front of the safe. Searching further, she removed the bag of gemstones. Coins, jewelry, banknotes, all noted and placed on the floor sequentially, in neatly stacked piles. When she had cleared out the whole safe, she started pushing on the inside. Nothing on the bottom, nothing on the right, nothing on the left. With the growing frustration, she turned her wrist and pushed the top of the inside of the safe. Another click.

She smiled again and palmed what fell from the hidden compartment.

Suddenly she heard a muffled groan from behind her. He was waking up — she didn't have much time.

One by one she placed the items back inside the safe, closed the door, and spun the combination lock.

"H — hey..." came from behind her.

Pocketing the object, she set the secondary lock back in place and turned around. Grabbing the two coffees sitting on the floor, she jumped back onto the bed.

Mental note: add another milliliter to the mix before adding the cream. He was supposed to be asleep longer than that.

Clearing her throat, she whispered out, raspy and sultry, "Hey, sleepyhead. Looks like someone finally passed out huh?"

"Rrrr... Rose? Yeah, I... I just rested my eyes... I don't..."

She smiled and handed him the coffee. "Third time's the charm."

She purred in his ear, "Drink up, you need to replace all the..." she glanced down at the crumpled, sweat-covered sheets, "... water." Purring the "R." She playfully tipped the coffee into his mouth. Groggy but clearing, he started drinking. She counted to herself.

He slowed down drinking and closed his eyes.

"... and five," she finished her count aloud.

He fell back on the bed, eyes rolling back to white, and passed out.

"Jesus, that took forever."

Rose drank the rest of her coffee in one gulp and started to get dressed. The room was strewn with clothing, food, and sex toys, the remnants of a morning of indulging the senses.

When she collected her things, she reached for her phone and cleared her throat. The line picked up.

"Yes?"

"I've got it," she said, pulling the USB drive out of her pocket, and gazing at it nonchalantly.
"The payment is waiting for you." The line went dead.

She went back over to the man on the bed and checked his pulse; slow, but stable. He would be fine. She kissed him on the lips, and ran her hand up and down his chest, remembering how his hot skin felt as it rubbed against her back. "Maybe I should have gone for four."

She grabbed her gear and headed out.

Have You Seen the Light?

"Have you seen the light?"

Images flickered across the screen in an ever-increasing tempo. They were filled with young, happy, healthy people having the time of their lives: dancing in clubs, snorkeling, playing golf, and drinking in bars. The images were permeated with the vibrancy and strength of youth, with an accompanying heart-thumping soundtrack. Interspersed with images of the Greek god Prometheus bringing fire from Olympus to the throngs of humanity. But this fire glowed green, in the form of an LED light. Above this cacophony of images and sound a husky female voice, with the slightest Chinese accent, provided commentary.

"Have you seen it? Have you finally freed yourself from the chains of carrying your communications device? Freed yourself to live the life you have always wanted? Freed yourself to the possibility of true communication?"

The screen displayed a particularly erotic clip of two people under the covers in a dimly lit bedroom. Six green lights were visible moving under the sheets. They blinked in a rapid, random fashion.

"All you have been waiting for can be yours. The new Prometheus GX, the most powerful personal communications system ever made."

The screen switched to a beautiful tropical beach scene, as crystalline blue waves crashed on ivory sand. A tall, slender, ethereal Asian woman clad in a gossamer silver toga sauntered into the frame. She spoke in the voice of the narrator.

"C'mon, see the light," she smiled happily, bordering on mischievously, and turned her head so her right temple faced the camera. On her temple, visible under the skin, were three green lights in a half-moon design, flashing in a random pattern. The screen faded to black, but the lights remained. Under the lights, deep red letters resolved into view. They read: "See the light. Prometheus GX."

A young man stared at the monitor, the only source of light in the room. Drawn curtains and heavy carpets muffled all sound.

"Justin?" A woman's voice called.

No answer.

"Justin? Honey?"

Still no answer.

The door to the room opened, and Justin's mother walked through.

Justin sat in front of his desk, slumped in his chair staring at the screen, frustration and longing on his face. The screen still displayed the end of the commercial, and the price, "Only $2000 USD", pulsed like a slow breath.

"Sweetheart?" Justin's mom tapped him on the shoulder.

He turned around, not the least bit startled. He grew used to being snuck up upon since the accident. Justin wondered how long it would be before she realized he couldn't hear her. After a moment she stopped talking and smirked at him. He reached up and switched channels on his cochlear implant. The sound of the non-electronic world leapt back into his mind.

"Sorry, Mom." He smiled.

"That's okay," she said, then smiled back and opened a window to let the warm summer air into the room.

"You should get out sweetie, it's a gorgeous day."

Justin glanced to the window, out over the emerald green grass, down the street to the sapphire ocean. The sun glinted on the water like pure gold, frothy wave crests caught the light and scattered it like a spray of diamonds. A brilliantly spectacular day, the first in weeks, waited outside his door.

He leaned back into the chair. "I don't want to," he whined, trying to shake off his frustration but pushing it more toward annoyance.

"I know you'd say otherwise, but you can't sit there all day. Go outside and get some air," Justin's mother commented, gazing down into the sparkling green eyes of her son.

A wave of anger rushed over him: he was far too old to be told what to do by anyone, even by his mother. He graduated college two years ago, the first in his family to do so. The world was in his hand! Practically immortal, indestructible! He whirled around in his chair fully intending to give his nagging mother the "look of death." He faced his mother, and the anger turned to guilt, and then to regret.

He sighed and stood up, then embraced his mother and kissed her on the top of her head. "Okay, mom. I think I'll go to the beach."

She hugged him tightly and smiled. Justin let her go, smiled, and then walked out of the room.

Walking past a hotdog cart perched precariously between the seawall and the street, he could hear its antiquated speaker push out a tinny commercial; advertising for one of the local surf shops, the one that sold him his ill-fated surfboard. The only one in the shop painted with a design of a Mako shark and flames. He bought it without hesitation.

Then he remembered the accident and the fact that what he heard was an approximation of the commercial as interpreted by his implant. Anger grew within him again, and he quickly ran around the sea wall and onto the dune, nearly knocking a wayward toddler to the ground.

He brushed his sandy brown hair out of his eyes and looked out over the water to the horizon. A beautiful southern New Jersey day greeted him, perfect in his estimation. The ocean waves were breaking ten feet out at about three feet high. Perfect for body surfing or to take out a boogie-board. The waves were filled with families and children enjoying the surf, erasing their cares of the world, at least for the weekend.

In the midst of all this activity and enjoyment he realized hardly anyone spoke to each other. For a moment it perplexed him, and he stood on the dune trying to ascertain the situation. Then he realized why. Nearly everyone on the beach bore the unmistakable LEDs of the Prometheus GX.

Groups of girls "Xed" (as it was called) to each other about groups of boys, of course, the boys were doing likewise about the girls. Couples Xed to each other as they lay in the sun, and families were communicating in vast groups of frenzied LED lights. The only sound of human activity on the beach was the occasional whistle of the lifeguard and the startled glee of children fearing the next wave.

Justin sat down on the dune, as far away from the shoreline as possible. "It's that damn commercial," he muttered to himself. As if on cue a young woman walked by and smiled at him.

"I wonder if she tried to X to me?"

A particularly large wave began to crash, and he followed it in time to watch it break. "Nice. That would have taken me all the way up the beach."

Justin's implant restored full hearing to him, but he so badly damaged his nerve could not provide any "enhancements." He learned to interpret the digital signals as sound, and if he didn't concentrate on the artificiality of it all, it sounded real to him. Of course, the GX needed to interface with the auditory cortex, the speech center, and his motor nerves which proved impossible given his "low bandwidth." Stem cell research had come a long way, but repairing cranial nerves remained stubbornly out of reach.

Since the completion of his physical therapy, nothing prevented him from hitting the waves, but he couldn't bring himself to go into the water again. He felt frail, shattered, and worst of all — merely human.

A group of young women ran by and one slyly glanced at him, pretending not to be interested; although her temple LEDs betrayed her and flashed feverishly. He turned his head so she would see the left side, and pretended to "X" to someone else. How could she possibly want someone like him? The two years since the accident had seen Justin grow pale and put on weight. He felt isolated and betrayed by his own body; when he finally escaped from his silent isolation by his cochlear implant, the GX came along and chained him to the rock of isolation yet again.

"Why the hell did I come here?"

He got up and turned to storm off the beach, but stopped in mid-stride. As far back as he could remember, he would never leave the beach before walking down to the shore and getting his feet wet, no matter how brief his visit how cold the water.

The weight of the past bore down on him, and he turned to the shore and walked down.

He skirted two sandcastles, and narrowly escaped stepping on someone's buried father. Finally, he made it to the wet sand.

The cool water lapped at his feet, and he felt the sand shift underneath him as the retreating waves pulled the land into the sea. He stood for a moment, staring at the water playing around his buried feet and his pale legs. He couldn't believe he would never go surfing again, yet secretly he also refused to believe his insecurities would keep him from doing so. He took a breath and scanned the horizon one last time.

The people on the beach were facing out in the same direction. He thought a pod of dolphins was swimming by, or a hydrofoil skimmed by past the beach. A replica clipper ship decked out with full regalia passed by daily, its white sails billowing in the wind, but it never caused much commotion.

His eyes darted back and forth again, sure that whatever the excitement, he had not noticed it. Once again alone and out of touch, he felt inferior. He decided to head back to the house and lose himself in the electronic world, the world where the limitation of his handicap was not a burden.

Justin waddled through the soft warm sand past a family similarly transfixed. Their LEDs glowed a steady bright green, and all of the beachgoers were in a similar state, all transfixed, LEDs solid green.

He sat down in front of the mother of the family and waved at her. No response. He snapped his fingers and said hello. Still nothing. As a last resort, he grabbed her shoulders and shook her; when she recovered, she refocused on the horizon and returned to her state. This time, however, he saw her lips were moving.

He focused on her suntanned face, studying her movements. After the accident, Justin's doctor suggested he learn to read lips, in case his implant malfunctioned. In mid-sentence, the woman mouthed a string of numbers. Leaning over to the father, who was similarly motionless, Justin pushed him by the shoulder. When he recovered, the father began mouthing numbers as well. He turned back to the mother, and as she finished the sentence he made out the words… "Pamrapo Bank, Bayonne, New Jersey."

"Those are bank account numbers!" Justin stood up and scanned the beach. "There must be four hundred people here."
Surmising from his computer science education and from what he knew about the system, for someone to hack into this many units

they would need to control them either at the microwave towers, or from someplace close by, but high up. He knew no one could have broken into the Coast Guard base and commandeered their towers, so it must be somewhere on the beach. He thought the beachfront hotels were too far away for use; the lifeguard stands were occupied by the lifeguards who were likewise frozen. Everyone old enough to use the device moved out of the water to the beach and sat staring at the horizon.

Glancing back out at the ocean, he saw the clipper ship anchored past the breakers. He looked up the mainmast, toward the crow's nest where a figure faced the beach. Justin squinted against the sun to get a better view, but he couldn't make it out clearly. Knowing he could be under surveillance; he ran over to a lifeguard stand as quickly as possible hoping he would not be noticed.

He snuck behind the stand, took the binoculars off the side, and examined the ship. In the crow's nest stood a young, pale male with a laptop perched on the rail. Dressed in the uniform of the food servers on the boat, the hacker turned north along the beach and hadn't noticed Justin run to his present location.

Justin surveyed the waterline. The waves were calm, but still potent, and the tide had come in. His palms began to sweat, and his heart pounded. For a moment he stood frozen in his indecision. His legs felt like lead. He recalled the feeling of water filling his lungs and sand tearing at his flesh. He heard the deafening roar of water and his panicked splashing as he tried to get his head above the waves. He could feel the crushing weight of the Atlantic Ocean beating down on him and its indifference to anything but the moon and sun.

Suddenly, he heard a little girl wailing from the unresponsiveness of her parent. Two more babies caught on. He scanned the shore and the boardwalk; the lifeguards were unresponsive, the security patrol likewise frozen. Everyone on the beach remained rigid, frustration and confusion etched into their faces. Everyone except him. There were two choices: ignore it and head home hoping the hacker would only take money and none of the children would be hurt; or swim out to the ship and stop him.

Back at the ship, the hacker scanned the south end of the beach. Justin had to act. He grabbed the lifeguard's rescue floater and raced for the shoreline. He knew the hacker would probably see him as he swam with the orange floater toward the boat, but he had to chance it.

He caught a break and hit the water as a large wave passed. The undertow helped him get past the first row of breakers without incident.

The second series of breakers did not go as well. A wave crested three feet over his head. Unaccustomed to the buoyancy of the floater, he tried to dive under the wave, but it carried him back up to the surface.

He opened his eyes in time to see the sunlight refracting through the wave in a brilliant display of grey, green, and blue. He managed a gulp of air, and then the wave hit him. The crest caught him squarely on the head, with the force of what felt like a hammer. He could feel the pressure on his cranial joints, and the spot where his cochlear implant entered his skull. He could also feel his old fracture throb, and he could swear he felt it shift under the strain.

In an instant all of the sensations of the accident came back to him: the feeling of his feet being ripped off the sandy ocean bottom as he miscalculated the wave, then the horror of feeling the back end of his board catching on the sand, his back flexing the wrong way as his body fought against the pressure of the wave and the resistance of the board. The absolute shock of his vintage 1973 "Ole" board breaking along its midsection; the confusion of tumbling over and over with the broken sections as the wave smashed him on the beach, slamming his head against the tip. Then the oblivion of unconsciousness.

Justin opened his eyes as he drifted on the surface clutching the floater. As the wave roared to shore, his head throbbed, but otherwise he felt fine. He looked back, where the people were still frozen in place, with some children recklessly playing in the waves. He turned toward the boat, only ten feet away but because of his angle, he could not see if the crow's nest contained an occupant.

Once he swam over to the ship, he looped himself through the strap of the floater and searched for a way onto the boat. Close to the gangway port, a mooring line drooped lazily in the water, he grabbed the line and heaved himself up.

Slowly he climbed up the line, his bare feet slipping on the varnished hull, until he made it to the gangway. Once on deck, he felt like a pirate raiding a pleasure yacht. The deck, filled with people who paid large amounts of money to sail on this boat from its homeport in New York City to Philadelphia, had the eerie silence of a funeral. Dropping the floater, he ran along the deck toward the bow, sidestepping well-dressed partygoers, who were staring directly up at the crow's nest.

He must still be up there, Justin thought, and jumped onto the rigging, climbing as fast as he could.

As soon as he cleared the rail, he missed a line and lost his grip, and accelerated toward the deck. He could feel the wind rushing past his ears and the sickening feeling of gravity pulling him down. Desperate to stop himself, Justin threw out his legs and arms, hoping to catch some of the rigging before he hit.

His left foot caught a rung and his leg strained under the force with increasing intensity until he felt his knee pop. The pain shot up from the joint and raced through his body; a deep pain, both dull and excruciating.

With immense effort, Justin kicked his left foot out of the rigging and slammed down on the deck. Instantly, he bent his leg, snapping his knee back into place, and the sharpness of the pain lapsed, and the dull ache remained. He lay on the deck for a moment, catching his breath and rubbing his rapidly swelling knee.

"I'd stay down there if I were you!" the hacker called down from the crow's nest. To Justin, the voice sounded distant and tinny. He reached up and tapped his implant's interface; it sputtered and fizzled, but didn't improve. He must have damaged it in the fall, and he hoped the external microphone was broken and not the connection to his cortex.

Justin scanned up the mast and saw the hacker staring down at him. The hacker displayed a large tattoo on the side of his shaven head; an eagle, its talons extended in anticipation of a kill. The LEDs of the hacker's GX flashed from the tips of the talons. He smiled mischievously and spat down at Justin. Fortunately, the wind blew it away from him.

A wave of determination rushed over him as he struggled to his feet, resisting the temptation to cry out from the pain. He put some weight on his foot, his knee felt stable enough to stand on but swelled badly.

The hacker growled down at Justin, "I said stay there!" He shook his head. "You must be stupid. I can do this forever and you'd be torturing yourself." He started frantically typing on his keyboard, not taking his eyes off Justin. "Don't say I didn't warn you."

Several people slowly and deliberately fixed their gaze on Justin. They focused on him, but their expressions were of pain and fear. Pushing off with his good leg, he leapt back onto the rigging to climb to the crow's nest. His knee seared in protest but remained steady. He brought his right leg up to the next rung when a hand grabbed his left leg. Justin saw a well-dressed man clutching his left calf; the man's face twisted with frustration.

Two more people shambled toward Justin. Holding onto the ropes with his hands, he kicked the well-dressed man on the forehead who let go and fell to the ground. However, the other two reached him and grabbed his feet before he could get them back into the ropes. He wrapped an arm through the rigging and kicked his right foot enough to throw off the latest attackers.

Justin started scrambling up the ropes as fast as he could; when he scanned around again, the passengers on the deck lurched toward him.

The hacker intensely pounded on his keyboard, sweat pouring from his face.

The rigging began to sway violently as the people grabbed it and shook, and Justin resigned himself to holding on as long as possible.

"He can't keep this up for long. He can't!" Justin spoke, clutching tighter as a particularly strong shake almost tossed him from the rigging. "I can't either."

Justin heard a scream from the beach and threw his glance over to the shoreline. People all over were breaking free from their trances and quickly coming to terms with the events of the last few minutes. Chaos ensued as parents scrambled for their children and youths tried to make sense of their trusted technology's betrayal.

The rigging stopped shaking, and Justin looked down to see the people struggling with their bodies, trying desperately to break out of their Prometheus-induced trances.

"He's losing control."

Justin started climbing the rungs again.

"He must have overloaded his system trying to move all of those people."

The hacker typed furiously and cast fearful glances down the mast. He entered a sequence in his laptop, closed the screen, grabbed the transmitter, and climbed out of the nest. A sudden cacophony from the beach peeled through the air as the security guards and lifeguards attempted to restore order.

Justin changed direction and climbed around the rigging to the other side, as the hacker passed by on his way down. He knew the hacker wanted to get below decks and blend in with the other hired hands. Only Justin would know who he was, and with his bad knee, he would never catch up before the hacker hid and disposed of the evidence.

In a flash, he remembered the family on the beach. He knew if disturbed, people would briefly come out of their trance, their limbs spasming as their nervous systems reasserted their control.

Justin launched himself out of the rigging and hit a group of twenty-somethings, knocking some of them to the deck. He landed on his right side and slammed his head into the planks. He completely lost all sound and his right eye started twitching. The group of passengers struggled to their feet, their LEDs flashing feverishly. In a circular pattern from the group, the people on the deck sprang back into life. The swell of activity overwhelmed the hacker, and he fell to the deck; knocked by a flurry of confused bodies, the laptop and transmitter scattered away from him.

Justin pulled himself on his feet and threw himself at the hacker, landing on the other's legs. They wrestled for a moment between the legs of frightened and confused passengers; kicking and punching and each trying to keep the other from standing. Finally, he flipped the hacker onto his back and punched him square in the face, knocking him unconscious.

"Lights out," he growled through a blood-stained twitching smile, although he didn't hear himself at all.

The warm autumn air caressed the beach, and the golden sun shone through a serene blue sky. The tourists from the cities finally left, and the locals enjoyed having the beach to themselves once again. A beach umbrella held watch over two blankets and a cooler of drinks. On top of the cooler lay the user's manual for a brand-new cochlear implant. A portable radio held it open to the 'Water and Your Ecotronic Cochlear Implant' section. A news broadcast played.

"... Prometheus Industries issued an emergency patch to fix the security hole. The hole could be used to seize control of the user's nervous system and cause the user to give information against their will. The company stated the devices have never been compromised in testing, but third-party applications could exploit it. Currently Prometheus Industries stock is at a ten percent loss in late-day trading... In environmental news, atmospheric carbon dioxide declined today for the first time..."

A loud wave broke on the beach, past the empty lifeguard stand. Justin stood up and extended his hand to help someone out of the water. He pulled a young woman in a black bikini to her feet and smiled at her.

"You ready to hit the next set?" he asked her, smiling broadly.

"You bet!" She responded and held up her boogie board.

They turned toward the waves and ran into the water.

He wore a brace on his left knee and carried a surfboard under his right arm.

The Greenhouse

Since that day twenty years ago, I have realized how much noise permeated the world then. Cars, planes, trucks, lawn-care machinery. Always screaming, always demanding my attention, with the not-so-subtle counterpoint of someone else trying to be heard over the din.

Then there were the lights. Always on, always shining. Making us think the world was so much safer. Any hint of darkness terrified most people to the point they forced the night to be as bright as the day.

The heat. It was impossible to forget the unrelenting heat. We never saw snow anymore and it never went below freezing.

We were careening on a runaway train, a relentless fall into an uncertain future with no control. Smothering ourselves in our waste and fiddling while the world burned.

I didn't miss the old world. I loved being able to look up at the night sky and see the Milky Way stretching overhead again. Like when I was a boy in the country. Brilliant blue and green with the occasional reds and oranges. That is what we lost in the time before. We lost our connection to the universe and traded it for jets to Machu Picchu, wall-to-wall carpeting, unlimited streaming services, and hermetically sealed forced-air office parks.

Sure, there was a hefty price for that change. But it was what it was.

Lying there, in the crunchy leaves of that late November day, peace settled across me and my home. Finally. I heard the animals of the forest getting ready for bed; robins twittering, squirrels jumping through the underbrush, a deer in the distance, snorting loudly and stomping to scare me off. In the house, my kids played games and popped corn by the fire. I could feel the temperature dropping now that the sun dipped below the trees, feeble orange rays piercing the gathering darkness. The tip of my nose grew cold, and I pulled up my woolen scarf. So quiet. I closed my eyes and let the cold sink into my skin, remembering my life before…

"Hey there, friend," spoke a voice from behind the tree in my backyard on that insanely hot September day. I wasn't sure at first if I heard it over the traffic from the road. I had finally gotten around to watering my tomatoes after neglecting them the whole day. My days blended back then, always busy rolling a stone uphill. It wasn't like I needed the tomatoes for survival, luckily. A hobby with a purpose I convinced myself.

"Hello, friend," I heard again from my right, sure an actual human voice called to me.

I put down my hose and turned toward the voice, looking around the trees to make eye contact. The house next door changed occupants so often in the 2020s that I was used to not being able to recognize voices.

"Hello?" I called into the air and smacked a mosquito that was sucking on my arm, the sound echoed off the tree in front of me.

"Horrible, aren't they?"

"Umm, yeah, invasive bastards," I glanced up from the carcass on my arm, the white and black stripes of the tiger mosquito now streaked with blood. I still couldn't see where the voice came from.

"I can't see you," I called into the air scanning around the trees but not finding anyone. I shot a glance at the windows of the neighbor's house, all of them were dark except the one over their sink. I'd been in that house nearly every time it changed hands, I knew it almost as well as mine. They weren't home.

"I'll be along soon, but I want you to consider something first."

I stopped moving and stood my ground, I knew I was being toyed with, and didn't like it. Still, I had no idea where this voice came from and I couldn't back down. I looked around the yard to the other houses. All of them were lit in one way or another, but nothing moved in the swelter. The hum of air conditioners and traffic drowned out everything else. The voice felt close, and familiar somehow.

My chest tightened and my hand shook. You don't screw with me at my place.

"You can't offer me anything, friend," I said with an acid bite. "I don't give people power over me."

"That is precisely why I'm offering it to you."

I swatted another mosquito, "Ha! Whatever, let's hear this offer." Already tired of dealing with this idiot, I wanted to end the charade.

The voice called, behind me now, and I spun around to look at the oak tree, whose ever-present stillness and strength radiated comfort to me.

"You'll like this, I assure you," it said calmly. I couldn't figure out gender, not high like a female, but not deep like a male either.

I stepped quickly around the oak tree, sure I would catch the person.

Nothing.

"What the hell?" I said, losing my patience, "I will beat the shi-"

"Please, there is no need for violence," now the voice came from my greenhouse.

Turning my head, I peered through the gathering dark; a figure stood in the middle, small enough to stand up full height in the six-foot glass building. I squinted, trying to make out the shape; it was getting so hard for me to see at night now that I passed forty.

With two bounds, I stepped up to the door, hoping to catch the intruder before it could run out of the only egress. The figure stood among the potted cacti and orange trees in the fading grey-green light, its face shadowed by the beams of the peak in the roof.

I took slow breaths and waited for its next move. Normally, an intruder would be a kid screwing around, at best, or a transient from the highway, at worst. Unless they had a gun, I wasn't too concerned. I had half a foot on it, and this wasn't my first tangle with a stranger.

"Good, now we can talk," it said, not moving.

I reached inside the door for the power strip that turned on the lights.

"The light won't work. Don't be concerned, it's not broken. I need anonymity to make my offer."

"Okay, since I have you trapped in here, let's hear it," I said and looked down at the figure's pale hands; no weapons, no jewelry, no tattoos.

"Excellent!" it said, with a definite chipper upturn.

I wiped the sweat off my forehead.

"This is it," the figure said quickly, not waiting to take a breath, "the heat, the invasive species, the famine, the wars, all the suffering, all of it."

"I've been working my whole life to reverse all of this. You're not telling me anything I don't already know here." I spat, my patience hinging on one misplaced comment which I knew would send me toward the figure to throttle it.

"I know. My offer is simple," it spoke, pausing for effect. "I will change the planet to how it should be. I will end climate change, stop all the exploitation of resources, remove those who would destroy for their gain, and I will add lasting peace and a United Earth. Everything exactly as you want it to be. How it needs to be. How... you... need it to be."

I stood, confused at what I heard. Usually, street people asked for money, for food, or to get home. Of course, I knew it was to get their next hit of oxy. They never wanted to bring ecological renewal and save the world.

"What?" I managed to choke out, shaking my head in disbelief.

"I told you you'd like this." Again, it paused for effect. I didn't like that this shadow figure had me so entranced, but I had to admit it knew how to create dramatic tension. "I can give you everything you've devoted your life to. All of it."

"How? You're a crazy dude in my greenhouse, how can you do all of that? How can I...?" With the realization deals usually have a price, I paused.

"What's the price? My soul?" I asked. Yeah, just an oxy head.

It laughed ever so softly, "You are a funny man. Why would I want the soul of such a forward-thinking person? Besides, what you're asking requires more than one soul. Many more."

Right there I realized I was dealing with a crazy person.

"Really?" I said coolly, and stepped back, resting my hand on the axe I kept just inside the door.

"Yes, I could do all of this on my own, but I can't get started without someone agreeing to the price. I have books to keep."

"The price is?"

"How much do you think it's worth to save the planet? How much has been lost because of humanity's bad decisions? What price saving our only home in the universe?"

Despite myself, the numbers leapt into my mind. I knew from the mountains of scientific data our culture skewed into this lifestyle after the Second World War. We'd grown decadent, wasteful, arrogant. There were too many people, wanting so much more than the planet could give. It was taking far too long for our numbers to drop, and far too long to wean ourselves off the drug of excess.

"Let's round that number down, shall we?" it said, knowing what I did. "Six billion. It's a nice even number."
Shocked, I inhaled quickly but stopped myself from reacting more. Losing six billion people would take us down to two billion. It's exactly the population that would allow the planet to heal the fastest. Compact and sustainable. Would they just 'go away'? Or did it have other plans? I shook my head in disbelief again and took up the axe in both hands, blocking the doorway.

"As I said, there is no need for..."

"Violence?" I shot back. "You're talking about murdering six billion people and you're lecturing me on violence?"

"They are dead already. And you know it. They will slowly die while watching the world burn around them. I'm only proposing to make their deaths quicker and start the healing process sooner. I need you to say the word."

The axe shook in my hand, and I hoped the figure couldn't see my face in the dark.

"I'm going to give you thirty seconds to get off my property. Then I won't call the police, I'll kill you myself."

The figure kept on speaking, ignoring my threat.

"Imagine how quickly the world would heal after it was over? Another 'Anthropause'. It's what you want, isn't it? It's your dream. In those dark, quiet nights when you are lying alone in bed, wondering where it all went wrong. When all the sacrifices you made seemed worthless. You got nothing but a warmer planet and an empty house. No one listened to you."

The axe fell from my hands.

"Yes, it is what you want. You can't deny it," the figure stepped nearer to me in the darkness. "Let me fulfill this one dream, one that can make your life not seem like wasted time. You can finally have control."

Somewhere in the back of my mind, a voice jumped to the front; yes.

I shook and my heart pounded. This was insane. I pushed that impulse down as fast and as hard as I could. I had to get rid of this person. I never wanted to think of this again. I steeled myself and leaned in.

"Sure, buddy, kill six billion people. Now get out of my yard and go back to whatever hellhole psych ward you belong in."

I stepped out of the doorway, signaling I had finished talking. With menacing slowness, it stood fully upright. It had been hunching the whole time. As it strode toward me, I focused on its head, still trying to see its face.

As it stepped through the doorway it met my gaze, just as the streetlight outside my house cast a blue light across its face.

"You agree! We have a deal then," he said with a smile, from a mirror image of my face. My eyes piercing into my own. Face to face.

I froze. The whole world spun around me. I realized then, what had I just done without thinking.

After that, he disappeared. I try to think of the last twenty years since then as a reset, and not "the collapse of society" as some people who survived like to call it. Nature simply started over, with some help. It's so much better now: the skies are clear, it snows again, there is more than enough food for everyone who is left.

We've gone all renewable, no fossil fuels. Trees everywhere. No meat. No poverty. No war. No more disease… well, after the last one anyway. It's better this way. It's so much quieter.

You may ask, Dear Reader, who I am? You all know me. I never lost control; I'm the man who sold the world.

When It Used to Snow in February

The kitchen bustled in full swing as the staff got ready for the dinner rush. Orders would start pouring in at any minute, and the more already prepped the better. Pots of pasta were at full boil, salads being cut, chicken and eggplant floured and breaded. The kitchen hummed with activity orchestrated over decades of practice.

A radio chimed out from behind a long metal counter. Covered in years of flour, and the occasional splatter of pizza sauce, the lone speaker was barely visible behind its white shroud. The pale pink light from the station dial glowed like the slowly pulsing heart of Frosty the Snowman. It never moved from this spot, and that is how everyone liked it.

"… previously, scientists thought the Earth was cooling off rapidly enough to plunge us into an ice age by the next century, but that theory is no longer supported. There is a possibility the opposite might be true, but it needs more study. Martin Jones, 1010 WINS, Washington."

The music switched back over to its regular programming and the mellow strains of Moonlight Sonata trickled from the speaker.

The cook glanced up from the counter where he made the latest in a series of pizzas started in the Nixon administration. The wind-driven snow blew past the glass door of the restaurant. He grunted quickly to himself, then got the sauce from the five-gallon bucket next to the radio.

With a long counter serving to separate the kitchen from the dining space, the 'restaurant' was nothing more than two Formica tables with simple wooden chairs and a hanging plastic menu board. Small and enclosed, it was always broiling from the heat of twin gas-fired pizza ovens right behind the counter. Both doors were always open: the one in the back of the kitchen, and then one in the front. Today, as a rarity, both were closed.

The front door swung open, dramatically, with an attendant frigid breeze. It flew so fast the bell over the door barely had time to chime before it slammed against the glass window and shook with an uneasy vibration. The cook called back to the kitchen and one of the part-time kids rushed out to push the door back into place.

"We might have to lock that," he sighed.

The kid ran back to the kitchen after being summoned again.

The next minute the door flew open again, slamming against the glass window. The cook was about to call back when he saw it wasn't the wind this time. Someone walked into the restaurant.

The figure struggled with the door to get it to close again. Fighting back the wind, it pushed it closed. Gloved hands covered in snow. No face visible. The cook, who had been readying himself to assist was impressed with the feat before him and smiled in admiration.

"Thanks!" He chirped with a grin and an upturn in his voice.

The figure turned back, and from behind a woolen hat and black scarf, both festooned with snow, a pair of hazel eyes smiled back. Quickly she took the scarf off being careful not to throw snow all over the floor. She had delicate features and a broad smile. Her eyes sparkled in the fluorescent lights.

"Oh, hi!" Instantly recognizing her, the cook welcomed the woman into the restaurant, although he did not remember her name. He glanced up at the order board.
"Yeah, uh, ten minutes." He gestured over to the table.

"Thanks, John," she replied, with a voice accustomed to instructing people what to do; confident, but relaxed. "Crazy storm, huh?"

John glanced up again, "I've seen worse. School gonna close tomorrow?"

She sat on one of the chairs with a sigh and didn't bother to look back at the windows.

"I've never seen one this bad before. Probably."

"So you get the day off?" he asked, taking a fresh ball of dough out and kneading it.

"I never get the day off," she joked, her eyes betraying a sullenness.

John nodded, knowing not to press an issue that might upset her.

Over the next few minutes, the activity in the kitchen never let up, and John kept apace with his endless pie-making. Customers started coming in, each of whom had their fights with both nature and an overly light glass door. Everyone had a silent fear the next customer would smash it to bits.

From behind the bustle of waiting customers, John called out to the woman at the table, "It's ready!"
He gestured over to the counter where a pizza box and white paper bag miraculously appeared on the counter.

She got up and pushed her way to the counter, as John rang up the bill, his floured hands deftly punching the numbers in on his cash register.

"$11.50," he called to her as she reached into her purse. She threw him a glance with raised eyebrows.

"Yeah, everything went up twenty-five cents. Blame Reagan."

She sighed and counted out the change with an assortment of dimes and nickels.

John glanced up as the door flew open yet again. "Hey, Doctor!" He said with a cheery smile.

Doctor? She thought to herself, turning around to see who this person - with the instant recognition amid the crowd - was. All she could see was a wall of bodies of those much taller than she. She turned back and handed the money to John.

"Hey John," she heard the voice of this supposed "Doctor" call back over the crowd. His deep resonant voice sounded embarrassed by the recognition.

She grabbed the pizza box and bag, pushed her way through the crowd, and out the door. An arm reached over the crowd and held it for her, while also keeping it from slamming into her face. She faced into the wind and started walking, head down, trudging through, her scarf nowhere to be seen.

Literally head and shoulders above the rest, the Doctor scanned the restaurant. It was packed, customers jockeyed for position, torn between dealing with the crush of humanity or the maelstrom outside. As usual, he leaned against the back wall, where the door would fly open if it were not for his foot - stealthily positioned to prevent just such a thing.

"Hang on!" called John from behind the crowd. In one motion he spun around, grabbed the pizza from the top of the oven, and then spun back to hand the box over the crowd. Again, with ease, The Doctor grabbed the box from over everyone's head with one hand, and with the other threw a crumpled $10 back to John.

"You owe me two bucks!" He yelled.

John nodded and grabbed another box for an irate customer who had been waiting for a while. They didn't understand the virtues of calling ahead.

The Doctor smiled and was turning to go when he saw a black scarf over the back of one of the chairs. Thinking quickly, he realized it must have belonged to the woman who just left, the one he held the door open for.

"John!" he called back. "She left her scarf." He gestured over with his head.

John nodded, he'd add it to the lost and found box. Whenever the rush died down.

The Doctor, who had never taken off his black stocking cap, tipped around the door and out into the blinding snow. He searched in either direction for the woman who left, but there was no sign of her. Even her tracks were gone in the spindrift.

The Hope of Water

Slowly, the robot inched its way toward its intended target, its black and lifeless eyes fixated on its prey. Trapped, and lit up by a blinding red light, the target could do nothing but wait for the inevitable as the robot crept ever closer; the sound of its servos moving its menacing arms permeated the air. Closer and closer it came.

Suddenly the bright red light turned off plunging its target into total darkness. The robot raced to where the target had been. In the dark, the eight-inch-tall robot crashed into the coffee mug. The two slowly tumbled together down the stairs into the basement, coming to rest on the soft carpet below.

"That's not very nice," said Eric Faulkner as he glanced up from his pack on the kitchen table.

His son Jason came back up the stairs, the quiescent robot in his hands, "I didn't mean it. I'm trying to work out its threat avoidance system, but it doesn't know what to do when I turn the targeting light off," Jason said, gently putting the armless mug down on the green molded epoxy table.

Eric cast a glance at the mug. "You need to be more careful. Someone always gets hurt when you let your excitement get the best of you. Okay, you know where the glue is, you fix it."

Jason walked out to the garage and came back a minute later with the ceramic glue. "How long are you going to be gone again?" He asked as he spread the glue on both ends of the handle.

"It should be a week, maybe less depending on how much we get done."

Jason nodded his head, "How is mom feeling about this?"

"The same way she always feels about these things, angry."

Jason pressed the arms of the handle together, making sure the seal clamped tightly, and then put the mug back on the table to dry.

Eric made note of the mug and cleared his supplies away from it on the table. "I don't want to take it by accident."

Eric pulled the reins on his excitement, "I guess I need to say goodbye to everyone then huh?"

"Umm, yeah," said Jason, with an "are you stupid?" expression on his face.

Eric set his pack down on the bamboo carpet and headed upstairs to the nursery.
He stepped into the room, soft pink light poured in through the windows. Smelling of hibiscus and lavender, the room had a womb-like feel – warm, soft, organic – that instantly calmed down adult and child alike.

He walked over to where his wife stood, gazing down at her daughter in the crib. He put his arm around her, and she softly pressed her body into his. "I'll never forget this sight," he said, as he gazed softly at his sleeping child.

"She just fell asleep," his wife, Janna, said, her voice barely a whisper. Eric rubbed her shoulder in response.

"Are you ready to go?" She asked, knowing the answer already.

"Yeah," he said.

Janna leaned forward and kissed the baby on its head. Eric followed suit, breathing in the smell of a newborn.

"See you soon," he whispered.

Moments later, Eric stood at the door to the garage. He hugged his son and turned to his wife.

"It will only be a week, don't worry. I'll be with James and you can always talk to me."

She tried to smile but quickly gave up this fruitless attempt. "James is a good guy, but it's not as good as being here," she wiped a tear from her eye. "Get your ass back to me as soon as you can."

Eric kissed her full on the lips, holding her for a moment, still passionately enamored with her, even after these fifteen years. "With a sendoff like that, how can I not?"

He walked back down the stairs toward the garage, his wife and eldest in tow. He smiled at them, kissed his wife again, and then closed the door to the garage.

When he stepped into the rover, it sprang into life: display panels lit up, fans whirred into life. He threw his pack on the bench and headed for the cockpit.

Eric sat in the captain's chair and strapped his four-point seatbelt on. His displays told him all his tanks were full, his suit stowed and in working order, guidance for the trip had been programmed, and all communications channels were open and functioning. He reached for the "hangar de-pressurize" button on his display, but suddenly caught himself, a wave of fear washing over him.

He unbuckled, scrambled over to his pack, and pulled the picture of his family from the compartment. "I almost jinxed this one."

Satisfied and calm, we walked back to the chair, strapped himself back in, and put the picture above the display panel. Then he hit the de-pressurize button. The rover rocked as the air rushed outside and the pressure equalized to the ambient. The garage door not only opened to the outside, but also out of his colony, past the city wall, concrete streets, and dwellings.

An hour later after driving faster than he safely should, Eric heard the rover's communications panel chime in, "Alexandria Research to Challenger One."

He fixed his eyes outside the window of the cockpit, seeing the vehicle guidance transponders trail off into the distance. He glanced down on his display, which showed a representation of his rover relative to a position off the screen. It read; "ETA, 21min."

"We have you en route with an ETA of twenty minutes. Confirm please," the voice chimed in again.

He checked his display. "Twenty minutes. Confirmed."

"Please use garage four. Welcome back."

"Alexandria, Challenger One. Will-do. Glad to be back. Out." Eric smiled.

As Chief Settlement Planner of Xanthe Terra City, Eric spent a lot of time moving from settlement to settlement. As his touchstone, he returned when he needed to rejuvenate his desire to create a unique culture, one that felt neither Terran nor Lunar: Martian.

"Hey, Eric!" A voice called to him from across garage number four.

Eric stepped out of the rover and shot a glance toward the access door.

"Hey, James!" He yelled back with a wave. "I was getting worried, you weren't banging on the window when I pulled up!" He said half-jokingly.

James Smalls had a somewhat annoying habit of always being at least ten minutes early. What Eric called "James Standard Time." Fortunately, James didn't mock others for not being as punctual as he, but his sunny disposition tended to make people feel guilty nonetheless. Being one of the first people born on Mars, before post-natal requirements came into full force, the spindly James stood in excess of seven feet tall.

"Good to see you! Is the air getting thicker up there?" Eric asked, a reference to the current terraforming efforts, to which he knew the reply.

"Air gets dense from the ground up, so you should know long before I do." The brown-skinned beanpole craned his head down, smiling.

James slung his bag over his shoulder and stepped up to the door of the rover, his enthusiasm, and impatience visible.

"Geez, so excited!" Eric laughed and opened the door.

Eric closed the hatch and stowed James's bag. James already called up the mission plan on the display panel. It played a recorded video, the Head of Exploration, Gina Bleyer briefed rest of the staff on the mission plan:

"Satellite imagery has shown us an interesting section of topography we had not taken in detail before." With her fingers, Gina moved the image on her display and zoomed in. "There is a series of small box canyons in this section of an alluvial fan one hundred clicks northwest of the research station. Spectral analysis is showing us high concentrations of hydrogen and oxygen."

Eric felt a surge of excitement.

"We weren't expecting water to start collecting here so soon after terraforming started, so we are thinking this might be an ancient aquifer and it may have started flowing to the surface again." She zoomed the photo in as close as possible. Box canyons, resembling holes in the ground from this perspective, were scattered in deposits left over from an ancient river delta. At the point where the closest canyon touched the delta, sunlight glinted off the surface. It could still be snow or highly polished rock, but the spectroscopic information had a strong indication of water.

"As usual," Gina continued, "our hydrologists are split between the Hellas Basin and the Northern Ocean and don't have time to come down to what may or may not be water," she looked up at the camera, breaking the fourth wall. "That's why we need you guys to go over and recon it, so we can give them our opinion on whether it is worth their time."

Eric leaned over and punched his much larger companion in the arm, giving a smile and thumbs up.

The route to the delta had been planned out, the rover packed, and the computer systems alerted to the transition. The rover would take over a day to get to the canyons, after which they would spend another three checking the area out, and another day back. It would have been easier if they had taken a hopper to jump the distances to the delta but again resources were needed elsewhere. They started rumbling off into the wilderness, sure they would at least see something no human eye had seen before.

Eric took the first watch at the controls. He wasn't exactly driving, because the guidance systems for Mars rovers had been perfected for at least the last hundred years. He merely paid attention to the sounds of any alerts from the control panels. For a few hours, transponders buried in the dirt road would steer the rover with barely any processing power used. The second half of the day would take them off the road close to their destination, and they would be driving over rough terrain toward the edge of the river.

After an uneventful drive overnight, the rover approached the delta just before dawn, as planned. They were both awake, having scheduled their shift changes to have them both fully rested when they arrived, as planned. James sat at the controls and rubbed his hands together in anticipation of taking it under manual control.

"Remember, this ain't no hotrod," Eric joked. "There is no mechanic out here if you break this one too."

"That wasn't my fault." He smiled in response.

The rover bounded off a slight incline and onto the river bottom.

The driving had been much smoother here than across the open wilderness. Water and wind kept this path clear for no one knows how long.

James maneuvered the rover down the riverbed; the canyon grew closer and larger as they rumbled along. Blessed with the first shift, which he won by besting James in rock-paper-scissors, Eric climbed into his suit, pulled on his gloves and boots, and stood up, swinging his helmet nervously in his hand.

"We aren't there yet," James said, glancing back and forth between Eric and the windshield.

Eric could barely contain himself from the excitement. He had gotten the extra sleep, eaten the extra rations, and if he didn't get outside and do something with all this energy, he felt he would burst.

The rover pulled up to the opening of the canyon as close as they thought they could safely go. Boulders and broken ground littered the opening where it connected to the riverbed, and even though the rover had been built tough, getting 'ledged up' and stranded was a risk they could not afford to take.

"This is as far as we go," said James, as he shut down the drive systems on the rover.

Eric already had his hand on the airlock door and waited for the rover to settle before throwing the switch.

"Take your time, remember the turn-back spot and the protocols," James said as he checked Eric's helmet for a good seal.

Reaching up to his wrist, Eric turned on the communication channel, which broadcast throughout the rover.

"Yes, I know. I will be careful. Geez, you sound like my wife," Eric smiled, as his helmet LEDs all turned green.

"Right, like I'd marry you," James mocked.

Eric, in an effort to merely test his gloves, raised the universal "reverse vee."

"The gloves are a good fit!" he joked.

When Eric finished checking all of his settings, he stepped out into the airlock, patting down his pockets one last time, to make sure all his tools were in place. "I'm good, be back soon."

James closed the door to the airlock, and then, Eric cycled the compressors. The external door hissed open, and the air rushed outside.

The airlock opened all the way and revealed the mouth of the box canyon. Eric analyzed his wrist display, which gave his position, the location of the supposed water, and distance. It calculated a half an hour walk, but he knew he could do it in twenty. Sensors on his helmet and throughout his suit were constantly scanning the surroundings and updating his maps. His suit's AI could stitch together a perfectly serviceable map from the ambient sound, but he would not be content to stand there and let it do all the work.

"Telemetry is good, signals are good, and updates are good," Eric said for the record. Quickly he checked the atmospheric readings. "Pressure is fifty-eight millibars and hydrogen has ticked up a few parts-per-million as well. There's something here."

James called back over his connection. "Be careful walking, there could be some mucky soil."

"I was thinking the same thing; the soil is probably sliding right off the permafrost." Eric walked down to the edge of the canyon wall and stared up at the edifice. Alternating rows of orange, ochre, red, brown, grey, and blue appeared to stretch into infinity above him. The wall climbed fifty feet high, imposing from this angle.

His Heads-Up Display popped over his vision, transparent enough to still see-through, but bright enough to give him useful data. His resolution increased dramatically and showed a flyover of his location in real-time 3D.

"Cool," James radioed from the rover. He could see everything Eric did, on another set of displays.

"Yeah, kinda scared me though, they need a warning when that is about to pop up," Eric replied.

"I'm sure the active sonar is going to love you when you start taking samples."

"Only one way to find out."

Eric reached into his pocket and pulled out his rock hammer. It wasn't as worn as some of the tools his geologist friends used, but he knew using it meant performing real science, not just moving numbers in some database. He took aimed for the corner of the nearest blue layer and swung. With a satisfying clang he could hear through his helmet, he contacted the layer and a small chunk fell away. He knew certain things about Martian rocks. In particular, he knew they usually contained the mineral hematite when formed in the presence of water. This piece had plenty of hematite 'blueberries' embedded in its structure. Again, his HUD popped up, and it gave him resolution down to the nearest millimeter.

He kicked up some of the sand at his feet, bone dry, like orange talcum powder. In fact, the whole area around him had the same aridity as any other place on most of the surface of Mars. A condition all of the people born on this planet were quite used to, most had never even seen naturally flowing water.

"Well?" Asked James from the rover.

"Dry."

"Martini dry or political humor dry?"

"Well, I'm not going to be filling up any swimming pools here."

Eric checked his gauges. He had four and half hours of air remaining, according to plan. If he planned to walk to the water and not worry about his oxygen the whole time, he had better get going.

He drew a deep breath, "Okay, I'm going in."

Eric stepped into the box canyon, his feet sliding on the orange regolith.

"GPS has got a good signal on you, no worries," said James, timing it to the instant Eric stepped into the shadow of the canyon.

Eric turned on his external helmet lights. "It's pretty rocky in here; the walls have been eroding for quite a while."

"When do you think was the last slide?" James asked.

"I dunno, everything has the same weathering pattern, but then again, all it takes is one global storm."

He scanned around at boulders and tried to match them to spots on the walls. He kicked a rock and his HUD updated his imagery. It showed him the layout of the next ten meters, layer densities of the rocks, the density of the air around him, and depth to the permafrost.

Nothing in all the data could tell him when the rocks last fell from the walls, or more importantly when it could happen again.

For the next ten minutes, Eric walked along the bottom of the box canyon. The dusty regolith gave way to thicker and more densely packed grains. He continually scanned for pressure changes in the air around him as well as hydrogen levels and humidity. Nothing fluctuated enough for him to take note.

Another ten minutes and he reached the spot he had been walking to see — his display synced with the maps he studied — and he knocked two rocks together to get the most detailed images he could. The ground had taken on a decidedly darker color, and the sand grains were packed tightly together. He knelt to see the ground closer. He imagined a torrent of water pouring out of the canyon as a spring rain washed down from the highlands.

For all the analysis and signs of water, nothing made itself known. The hydrogen levels did not change, humidity held constant and although the ground had become denser, whatever did it appeared to be long gone.

"Damn," Eric cursed into his mic.

"You've done half an hour of searching, what makes you think you'd find something so easily? They couldn't even prove water existed on this planet for fifty years." James counseled.

Eric sat down on one of the large boulders and looked up. Through the darkness, he could see the broad stretch of the milky white sky, running like an inverted river over him. All this new water had been expensively trucked in from the Belt or released from the permafrost. No longer was Mars' atmosphere pink, but white because of it. Finding an aquifer here would turn Utopia Planitia from a research base into a thriving city. He knew it had to be here; he had to find it.

Feeble sunbeams glinted across the top of the canyon, copper-colored and ephemeral. Eric checked his meter, he still had four hours of oxygen left.

"So, what do you want to do?" asked James.

"I'll stay in the area for a bit, might as well do some regular old science while I'm here. Besides I can…" Eric saw a red light out of the corner of his eye. Terrified and excited, he spun his head and glanced up the canyon, along the arroyo.

There, a hundred meters away, floated a red light. Eric scanned around the canyon walls to see if this could be a reflection coming from the top, or sunlight making it down to the floor and reflecting off some ice.

"Besides what?" James asked.

"Hold on, I see something here."

"See what?"

"A light up ahead in the canyon. Do you see it?"
James swung over to his other display, analyzing Eric's feeds, and checking his sensor data.

"Eric, I don't see the light you are talking about."

"You're kidding me, right? It's right there in front of me, a hundred meters. Red light, about a half a meter in diameter?"

"There's nothing there," James replied, his voice slowly showing his concern. "I see a photon cluster, but no electromagnetic signal. Are you sure there isn't light bouncing off something nearby?"

Again, Eric checked around for any possible light sources, but no sunlight came down into the canyon directly. Eric shut off his helmet light. The red light stopped moving but did not change in intensity.

"James, can you shut off all the external lights on the rover? I want to make sure there isn't anything bouncing off the walls here."

"Yeah, no problem."

The floodlights on the rover blinked out.

"Put the sunshield up too, while you're at it."

"Okay."

The windows of the rover turned black, keeping any light from making it out of the big windows.

The red light remained unchanged.

"How's that?" James asked.

"No different." Eric squinted his eyes, trying to see anything with mass at the center of the light. Nothing. He switched his HUD to read in all spectral bands, but the light showed only in infrared and visible. "I'm picking it up on infrared too, so you are telling me this gives off light and heat, but it doesn't have mass or a fuel source?"

"All I can tell you is what I see," James commented back, "it's plasma or some kind of out-gassing from the local rocks. Subsurface water could have stored methane as well."

"But you would be picking up carbon dioxide, no?" Eric thought he heard James sigh over the connection. "The atmosphere is mostly carbon dioxide remember. There is no way I can tell from the ambient, especially with all the fluctuations from the terraforming."

"Well, it has to be *something*." Eric turned back to the rover, perched on a rocky 'island' in the middle of the dry river.

"How's my beacon?" Eric asked, wondering if his identification beacon showed up in the rover.

James swung his chair over to another set of displays. It showed their position relative to the delta, the canyons, and to each other. Eric's beacon flashed a slowly pulsing royal blue.

"The satellites have you good. I can triangulate fine. One of your arms is shorter than the other?"

"Ha-ha," Eric laughed with no feeling. He turned back toward the red light. It floated at the mouth of a branch in the flat canyon, with high walls, and boulders scattered on the floor. He studied the rocks — there were plenty of spaces between them to walk through. He felt he would have no problem exploring it.

"I'm going to head in and check it out," he said.

"Of course you are," James called back.

"Like you wouldn't," Eric smiled, as he started walking to the mouth of the canyon, and as he did, the red light receded.

"Watch your butt."

Eric walked into the canyon, taking slow cautious steps. He knew he had a little less than four hours of oxygen in his tanks, and his re-breather could work for another hour before it became saturated. Still, he hoped he wouldn't need to worry, this light couldn't last long.

"What do you think it is?" James asked.

"Don't you remember something about plasma balls being caused by stresses in rock layers?"

"Yeah, but those are usually centered around earthquakes and fault lines. This section is, I believe, geologically inert," James replied. Geology always excited him more.

"Maybe the extra water lubricated some faults, and they are moving again?"

"Possible. If it was green, I would say methane outgassing as well."

"Swamp gas? Well, I guess it's possible, it could have been trapped in the permafrost and ignited when the oxygen levels started going up," Eric didn't believe his own ears though. "It isn't green. It doesn't seem to be moving fast either. It's localized."

"You want to follow it?" James asked.

"Why not? I have plenty of oxygen, we have good maps, and we did come out to explore this region, right? There is something here we didn't count on."

The communication channel clicked open for a few seconds; James's breathing could be heard in the background.

"I'll get my suit on," he said with finality.

"You can't," shot back Eric. "The plan is we always have one person at the rover in case something goes wrong."

Again, silence filled the communication channel.

"I swear if anything happens, I will kill you. You got that?"

"Nothing is going to happen. I have like four hours of oxygen left, it took me half an hour to get here, so I will go out another hour and come back. I'd still have at least an hour left. Okay?"

"Fine," James added curtly. "I can't stop you anyway."

Steeled in his decision, Eric started after the light. He took slow deliberate steps, watching his footing, and checking his location in the canyon. He set his map to trace his route so he could find his way back. A green line traced its way along the virtual representation.

The closer Eric walked toward the light, the further away it appeared. At least, it didn't get much closer. He checked his map repeatedly, and he finally reached the point where the light had been when he first saw it. He traveled one hundred meters, and the light appeared to be at least another one hundred meters away. Keeping pace with him.

"That's not right," he said quizzically.

"I know," James crackled over the communication channel. "Do you think it's something you are putting out, and the funhouse effect is making you think it's there?"

Eric quickly brought his wrist display up. Using three fingers on his right hand, he pressed the necessary contacts and shut his suit down completely. He saw the sky overhead and heard his breathing. One hundred meters distant the red light still hovered there, floating quiescently and pulsating.

"No, my friend, you are real," he said, boring his stare through his visor.

He scanned his display. The three buttons were glowing soft amber, barely visible. He pressed the three again and his suit sprang back into life.

"DO NOT do that again!" James's voice yelled into his earpiece.

"It's real James. Whatever it is, it's real."

"Then get back here, and we can call for a proper research team."

Eric completely ignored James, and walked toward the light, faster this time.

"Eric? Eric… answer me!" James pleaded, not hiding his frustration at all.

"I'm keeping my sensors on full broadcast. You can watch. I'll call you when I need you." Eric switched off his transmitter, cutting James's reply in mid-sentence.

Determined to catch up with the light, Eric started running toward it, sidestepping boulders, and bunny hopping as he went.

As fast as he ran toward the light it kept exact pace with him, never getting closer nor farther away. Eric reached a full-out run as the light receded around a bend in the canyon wall.

He turned the bend and stopped instantly. The light disappeared.

He scanned around frantically; he stood in a close canyon, ochre walls stretching up and meeting at the top, side channels branched out all around him, and the ground beneath his feet felt slippery.

Eric turned on his HUD, its image had low resolution. Frustrated, he reached down for a rock to give his active sonar something to work with, as he did the ground beneath his feet gave way with a loud *crack*.

Red light floated everywhere. Water gurgled. Tumbling and falling.

He opened his eyes and focused on the tiniest sliver of white light, high up and far away from him. The crack that opened under him was a thin layer of mineral rock. He figured he had broken through and fallen ten meters to the floor below.

He lifted his left arm to check his display panel, and a wave of excruciating pain shot through his body. With all the willpower he could muster, he flopped his arm onto his chest, crying out when it landed. The display panel had broken, exactly like his arm. He had no way of knowing where he was. James would know where he fell, and could probably figure out quickly what happened, but Eric could not expect the cavalry for at least an hour.

He calmed himself and caught his breath. At least his life support still worked properly, and the reactive fibers in his suit already splinted the break. He didn't feel any blood on his arm, and his vision fully cleared. "Sit tight," he told himself. "James will be here soon."

He saw the red light out of the corner of his eye. He turned his head; ten meters distant, it was much clearer, and yet no bigger.

"Bastard," he cursed.

Eric lay there for a bit, ruminating on the fact that sometimes exploring requires taking risks, and if you are afraid of those risks, then you should probably stay home and let someone else do it.

He landed in a small cave that had been a vernal pool at one point. The smooth floor had hematite blueberries scattered about it like a child dropped them but hadn't bothered to clean up. The walls, also smooth, curved gently up toward the ceiling, where they met the jagged line of the crack he fell through. They glistened, covered in condensed water, like morning dew on grass. He surmised the stream that ran through here probably detoured underground as the water table fell, leaving a weak layer of mineral deposits on the surface, like a crevasse in a glacier.

He stared at the ever-quiescent red light. It floated, motionless and pulsing slowly. As the shock of the fall wore off him, Eric could feel the ground vibrating beneath him. Not rhythmically, like machinery, but constant, with a somewhat predictable pattern. Eric smacked his right hand on the ground and his HUD sprang into life again. Instantly it displayed his environment: humidity at thirty percent, pressure at one hundred millibars, the temperature at three degrees Celsius.

The area sloped down gently about a hundred meters away from him, like a stream flowing to a lower location. Again, drawing all his will, slowly he stood up.

His vision greyed for a moment and then cleared. The floor did slope down, in the direction of the light.

"Well now," he said staring at it. "Lead on."

Taking baby steps — for he was no longer in a hurry — Eric inched his way down the slope. The light kept its fifty-meter distance at all times, always leading.

Eric's active sonar popped back on, updating and refining the resolution of his area. Data flowed in slowly at first; but then the trickle became a torrent. The HUD displayed the entire surrounding area in extreme detail, twenty meters ahead, it showed a smooth undulating line. This reading meant one thing. Water.

Slowly he walked down toward the water, taking small, sure steps. The light floated out toward the middle of the stream and hovered there. For the first time, Eric could make progress toward it. His arm ached and his head throbbed, but he peered as closely as he could toward his glowing companion. As before, it pulsed slowly and quietly, its only change: it finally stopped moving.

Even with the sonar, he could not tell how deep the water flowed, and decided not to test it.

"That makes sense," he said, staring at the light. "Salinity is probably high here too." He noticed white crystals lining the walls near the stream.

He stood for a moment feeling the steam vibrating through his feet. He had done it, he found the water. They could expand the city easily; humanity would have an even greater foothold on this barren world.

The joy of his discovery quickly began to fade, as did the light.

Watching the light fade completely, Eric's parched lips whispered the question, "You lured me, didn't you?"

When the light faded, he realized it was at the tip of something protruding from the stream. Brown and sleek, it looked like it either dripped down from the ceiling or grown up from the stream. His active and passive sonar sent back terabytes of data. It wasn't stone. It absorbed sound, as if...

As the thought entered Eric's mind, something grabbed his legs so forcefully they buckled and he collapsed onto one knee, sending water splashing. From the left side, something hit him in the head and dropped him to the stony ground, flipping him onto his chest and cracking his faceplate. Adrenaline pumping, he flipped back onto his back, ignoring the screaming blue-white pain in his arm. Another hit, this time across his faceplate. He heard air hissing, and a spider's web of cracks instantly grew across the glass. All of his helmet lights turned red, and a warning sign flashed above his HUD: Decompression Danger. Exposure Imminent. His suit's emergency systems spoke out the warning as well.

Another hit, this time across his chest, and he screamed in pain. His reactive suit stiffened in all directions, sensitive to the high G-forces hitting his body, protecting his bones and organs but rendering him motionless. His HUD flickered and flashed in his helmet as it did its best to interpret the data flooding into all the sensors in his suit. Another hit, and still another. Eric went numb from the pain. He could hear his oxygen pouring out into the thin air, his life slipping away with the precious gas.

Desperately trying to sit up and push away as best he could, Eric could see the formation reaching toward him. Rooted to the ground, it did its best to get close to him, but couldn't reach him. Brown tendrils exploded from the water hitting him over and over and pulling his legs.

In a panic, Eric started screaming, "James! James!" With each exhalation, he grew weaker and weaker.

The HUD flashed out. Eric could see drops of water on his

faceplate and cracks throughout. He looked through a hole in the faceplate and saw the moisture condensing as his air completely leaked out. He heard a clicking sound and a large splash as he felt himself being pulled into the frigid stream.

Eric's world turned red as his vision began to fade. Then to grey. Then to black.

Sagittarius

A rush of light filled George's vision. For the first time in three years, his eyes were open, and the flooding light overpowered his optic nerves.

Behind the glare, his mind raced with images. Scenes of strange grey humans, and more of the tall thin aliens with enormous obsidian eyes. He felt the pain and anguish of three years of a bloody and costly war. He could hear the death screams of thousands of combatants. He felt the joy of victory and the crushing loss of defeat. He saw the alien he met on Rebecca's Planet raise his blaster and fire over and over until the scenes faded back to white.

"Hello?" A soft female voice called out to him. Instantly he recognized it.

"Hello. It's good to hear from you again," he replied.

"Your name is Amy is it not?"

"Yes George, you know that," the voice responded pleasantly as if she knew he was teasing her.

"Where are you?" he thought.

"Earth, back at my parents' house. You must be close by."

"I don't know where I am yet."

An image of the young woman he saw on the fast transport to Earth flashed through his mind, followed by the titanic globe of the planet as he saw it through the observation window.

"I guess we aren't alone after all," she said with mixed relief and fear.

"No."

The image of the alien and the blaster flashed through his mind again.

George felt footsteps walking toward him. Another distinct voice, male this time, called out to him in his mind.

"Hello?"

"Hello," Amy responded. "It's okay George, you have a guest, I'll attend to our new friend."

The two voices disappeared from his mind. An emotion of gratitude filled him, and then a separate feeling of trepidation. He felt a new presence, physically near him. Then a second.

Finally, the presence came near, and he focused on it. With his eyes still too overloaded to see, he imagined a hospital room, with a single door. On the other side of the door Alyssa, his wife stood. She knocked quietly.

"Come," he called out in his mind.

A moment later he heard the physical sound of a knock on his door. The same knock he heard in his mind.

"Come," he called out again.

A pause, and then another knock, more pleading this time.

"Come in!" he called out. Why wasn't she listening?

Blurry shapes came to his eyes, blue-grey amorphous patches held motionless against a white background.

He imagined the room again and matched the patches to the bed and flowers scattered about him. The door opened and he saw Alyssa enter the room with a woman he knew to be his doctor.

There were no new patches in his vision, but they were becoming more distinct. He willed himself to see clearer, and in an instant, he had complete sight. Exactly like the room he imagined.

He heard the door open and Alyssa and his doctor walked in.

Instantly Alyssa flew to his bedside and threw her arms around him. He smelled her skin and inhaled as deeply as he could. He felt her strong arms squeeze his atrophied form and savored the feel of her flesh on his. He shut out the universe to feel her.

Then he saw her pull away from him with a concerned expression on her face.

"Can you hear me?" she asked.

A moment later she pulled away from him again, physically this time, and asked, "Can you hear me?"

"Yes. I can hear you," he thought.

Alyssa winced like she had been stung by a bee. She threw her hand up to her temple and pressed, squinting hard. The doctor made a similar gesture. She staggered back, her face twisted with fear.

"I can hear you. What's wrong?"

Alyssa dropped to her knees screaming in pain.

"What's wrong with her?!" his mind screamed.

Alyssa screamed again. The doctor clawed her way to the bed in an attempt to stand.

George saw a crowd of staff enter the room and drop in pain.

The next moment he heard the door open, and five nurses came rushing in.

"Help them! Something is wrong!" George thought with rising fear.

The nurses dropped, writhing in agony.

He sat bolt upright in bed, forcing his muscles to function as though he had not been lying in a coma for the last three years. Desperation rushed through him.

"I'm killing them," he thought, as a nurse stopped moving completely.

"You're right, stop thinking about them and physically speak," a third, unfamiliar voice spoke in his mind.

"I understand."

"I'm fine," George spoke aloud in measured, soft tones.

Alyssa, still squinting and in pain, struggled up to the bed.

He looked down at her and smiled, half of his face still limp so that the smile ended at the midline under his nose.

"I'm sorry sweetheart. I've missed you so much," he slurred out.

Alyssa smiled back, blood trickling from her ears, and then collapsed on the bed.

22:17

An incredibly long day finally came to an end for William: up at 05:00, slogging into work and spending the day staring at code. He'd been a developer for the last thirty-five years in some capacity. He needed a change of career, or a life less ordinary.

On the way back home at the end of the day, he fell asleep on the Metro. Twice. Luckily, he was at the end of the line and didn't have to pay much attention. Everyone on the train was either going to or coming from a New Year's Eve party — in various states of drunkenness.

When the train got into the station he sluggishly alighted and plodded to his car. It woke up before he got there; music playing, heated seats warming up, the heater warm, but not hot. He got in, drove the car out of the garage, and then let it drive him home.

Again, surrounded by technology, but he didn't mind this one so much as he could catch some sleep on the way home. Illegal yes, but he wondered how many drunk people would be driving tonight. At least here the A.I. focused more than a human could.

When he got home, William jumped on his exercise bike and loaded up the latest live class. An extremely perky young woman got on and started to audibly and visually get the class ready to go — he despised her perkiness. But to him, she was easy on the eyes and he partially enjoyed the voyeuristic thrill of watching, even if it didn't motivate him to pedal any harder. He hoped his connection wouldn't buffer again.

After the class, he showered, microwaved his dinner, and put on his favorite Netflix show.

His eyes drooping again, he glanced at the digital clock next to his 4KHD TV. It read: 21:36 12.31.2022.

He knew he wasn't going to make it, despite the cajoling and invitations he received on his phone.

One more cup of coffee heated up and drunk. At 22:17 he lost the battle with sleep and blissfully drifted off.

What felt like days later, his eyes opened to a stark bright light, and intense cold. He wondered if he'd fallen asleep with the lights on and forgot to turn on the heat. His house should have turned it on for him anyway. Power outage? Groggy, he lifted himself off the snow.

"… snow?"

William quickly glanced around, disoriented and confused. How could he be outside? It wasn't even cold last night.

As his eyes focused, trees filled his field of vision, and an orchard came into view. He stood in at least half a foot of snow, and his woolen socks were soaked through.

He recognized nothing at all as he surveyed the area. There were no roads he could see, even though he lived on a major six-lane road. No houses, despite living in a large development. He knew his area had once been an orchard, but that was back in the 1940s.

Shivering, he checked his body, he wore sweatpants, a hoodie, and nothing else. Both were emblazoned with his college alma mater. His cellphone was still in his hand; he'd fallen asleep with it. He fiddled with it for a few minutes, but it had gone quite dead.

"It's gotta be a dream…" he said to himself, inadvertently channeling Marty McFly.

It was too bright, too cold, and too painful to be a dream.

In the distance, he heard music playing. Not from a car or a stereo, but actual music. A piano. Distinctly.

He did his best to localize the sound and started walking through the snow towards it.

"Ragtime?" He said between trembling lips. His heart jumped and flopped in his chest.

He picked up his pace a bit; his feet were completely numb, and the lack of feeling let him move faster.

The sense of urgency drew him faster toward the music. He recognized it as "The Maple Leaf Rag" by Scott Joplin. Not a recording, a live performance. Embellishing and improvising as they played.

He crested a small hill and found himself on a dirt road. Opposite the road a barn stood. Not one with livestock, but hay bales, tractors, and machinery. No power lines ran to it. There were several Model T Fords parked outside, and two carriages with horses. His head swam and he started to lose his connection with reality. If this was his reality.

The music stopped with a flourish, and he could hear a crowd of people rise in cheer. It broke like a wave, and the piano started playing "The Entertainer" to rancorous applause.

Crossing the road and approaching the barn door, William slipped on something. He slammed into the snow with a thud. Searing from the pain, he reached down and grabbed a frozen newspaper, his icy antagonist. Flipping it around, he found the headline. "Alexandria Gazette, Wednesday, December 31st, 1919. Evening Edition"

William started laughing hysterically. He could not grasp the situation in front of him. On impulse, he gathered himself to his feet. Laughing uncontrollably, he did not notice when the music stopped, and hushed voices rushed out of the barn.

The gathered local farmers gasped at the appearance of this seemingly escaped mental patient. He was dressed in his pajamas, emblazoned with the name of the hospital he must have recently escaped from. The women, dressed in their Sunday best, huddled their children close, lest they should behold this madman. Several of the men were approaching William calmly, as they would a spooked horse.

"Easy there," one man whispered to him in a soothing voice. "We will get you home. Don't worry."

One of the younger men turned back to the crowd,

"Quick! Someone get Doc Peabody. Maybe he knows someone at this hospital! It's the State Penn!"

The Mesa

Tara's eyes followed the edge of the mesa as it stretched into the distance. Curving like a semi-circle, the soaring sandstone escarpment of the Vinson Massif rose above the cloud deck like a peach-colored island floating in a pearl-white sea. The startlingly blue sky arched overhead, endless and dominant, so much so she thought she could feel the weight of the ninety-five kilometers of air above her. Her oxygen mask helped her breathe in the thin, dry air.

This far above the clouds, no wind blew, no animals flew, and her ears were greeted with utter silence. The landscape had an alien feel.

Of course, it wasn't, climate change rendered this part of the world unrecognizable. A hundred years ago this landscape lay buried under a kilometer of ice and would have been entombed until the continents crashed into each other again in a few hundred million years — if humanity hadn't played with forces it did not understand. Since then, the polar caps melted and sea levels had risen seventy meters, giving the planet a completely different appearance, and exposing surfaces and anomalies never intended to mix with the genus homo.

Tara turned back around toward the helicopter, its slowly spinning rotors still bled off the momentum from carrying them from McMurdo City. Argentina recently began expanding its claims, and once the Antarctic Treaty was abandoned, the starting gun went off. The United States presumed control of the Peninsula, with McMurdo City being their beachhead. They feared SpaceX or The Solar Consortium would arrive soon and cause real trouble. Tara, lead explorer for the American team, came here to establish a presence as quickly as possible. She felt acutely aware of the pressure.

"Are we set?" She called to the tall man stepping away from the chopper, his bent frame barely clearing the blades.

"Yeah," he replied. Tara's sunburned face, oxygen mask, and goggles reflected in his shaded goggles. "The low cloud deck is dangerous. I hope that little stunt gives us time."

"If we're lucky." She grabbed her pack off the ground and took out the small United States flag threaded through the top straps. She reached up and tapped the camera on her own set of goggles.

"We claim Vinson Massif for the United States of America, in the spirit of international cooperation and peace."
Not believing the words coming out of her mouth, she heard the lines come out dull and flat.

She placed the weighted flag's base on the bare rock, its fifty-two stared banner hung slack in the breezeless air. She immediately shut off the camera.

"Let's go." She turned to face due south, toward the geographic pole.

The curling edge of the massif dropped off twenty kilometers away. They had to survey as much of it as possible, as quickly as possible. The summer sun rose with astonishing speed.

"GPS is tracking, satellite recording uplink is good." The man explained, tapping his goggles and scanning the landscape, "Fifteen degrees, sunny. Not a bad day." He adjusted his oxygen mask.

Tara, already ahead of him by several meters, didn't stop or comment. He ran up behind her, kicking pebbles as he went.

"Are you always so determined?" he asked her, pulling his pack tighter upon his shoulders, and bouncing in his steps.

"Yep."

He raised his eyebrows and pursed his lips nearly pressing them against his mask. "This doesn't have to be a death march. No one has seen this place without the ice on it — we're explorers!"

He genuinely did believe it.

Tara kept walking, without comment.

"You're gonna stay quiet the whole time, huh?" he asked, resignation creeping onto his face.

"Look," Tara barked, turning on her heel to face him, "I'm not here to explore. I don't give a shit about opening the frontier for humanity. This pays. Really well. I got a ton of bills and a brother stuck in a carbon sequestration debtors' prison in the middle of the ocean. We need to walk the surface so the GPS can track us and cement the claim for the Americans before the others show up, and that's what I'm gonna do. Now, less talk, more walk. Entiendes?"

In shock, he stopped walking, his red parka reflecting the baking sunlight. "Yeah." He stood still, waiting for her to resume her lead.

She took a quick breath, spun around, and started off again, her pace quicker this time; peach pebbles crunched under her boots and scattered in every direction.

"So what do I do if we see something?" he called after her.

She waved dismissively.

"Okay… I'll just note it. Yeah?"

Crunching boots.

"Yeah." He started walking behind.

After several minutes the ground smoothed out, nearly flat, with boulders breaking the monotony.

"This is a desert," he said, skipping over a knee-high rock.

Tara glanced down at her watch but kept walking.

"I wonder if… hey!" He called.

"What?" she barked back, not breaking her stride.

"There, in the hollow, do you see that? Pink slime?"

He stopped and pointed to a depression behind a sunbaked rock.

Tara stopped and leveled her gaze at the ground. The hollow held a pink substance, veins of orange decorated the surface. It motionlessly reflected the sunlight.

"Looks like fungus. Make a note, then let's go."

"No, not a fungus, more like bacteria. You know that pink stuff that grows on snow?"

"So make a note. I'm not stopping for a yeast infection."

He turned to her quickly, eyebrows furrowing, then stared back down into the hollow.

"Biology," he spoke into the air, commenting on the video. "We found this. I think it's bacteria. I've marked the location with GPS. I dunno, I think maybe Johnson or Briggs would like to check this out when we get back. Continuing on."

He reached up to his goggles and pressed the GPS button to record the location. Again, he had to run to catch up with her.

"Took care of it. I can't wait to study it."

Tara didn't comment.

As they walked away, the substance in the hollow moved, inching up the side before sliding back down.

After another five minutes of walking in silence, the surface leveled out completely again, but instead of stone, long, cylindrical blocks littered the landscape.

Tara kept checking her watch, trying to beat an imaginary clock before the weather cleared up and other interests arrived on the mesa.

"Cool!" He commented aloud. "Petrified logs!"

He completely stopped and sat on one of the ancient trees.

"These are *Glossopteris*. They have been extinct since the Permian. I've never seen a trunk before."

Tara stopped again, sighing loud enough to be heard through her oxygen mask.

"Aren't you the little scientist."

"Yes, I am as a matter of fact, and this is important because this species wasn't alpine. It shouldn't be here."

"Yeah, well, the world is a twisted place. I'm gonna keep going. Catch up if you can."

Tara hopped over another petrified log and skittered down a slope of rocks behind it.

"It's different over here. Be careful."

"I'm amazed you care," he said quietly, taking pictures with his goggles and noting the coordinates.

He walked after her, stepping over logs and scanning the area for anything unusual. Tara marched on, ten meters distant, her pace ever quickening.

With a bright flash of light, the scientist turned back north, toward the helicopter. The clouds below the massif cleared, and sunlight reflected off the stream in the valley below. He listened and heard other helicopter blades in the distance.

"We're not alone anymore."

Pulling out his tablet, he called up the GPS map and examined the outline laid by their traveling. A fraction of the area had been covered.

"Hey, Tara! I hear someone coming, we have to…"

He tripped over a log and landed on the ground with a loud crack, his oxygen mask tearing off his face and his tablet scattering over the pebbles.

He winced and reached down to his leg, feeling for anything broken. "I need to pay more attention here."

He got up and started towards her, bounding over the log she warned him about and slipping.

Tara stopped dead and listened, sure she heard the scientist call out for her a second time.

"Damnit, I can hear it too. Stop wasting time!" she yelled as she turned back toward him.

She could see clearly up to where she left him and could see the log she hopped over.

"Hey!" She called, forgetting his name. "Hey, let's go!" She searched around the area but could see no sign of him.

"I swear, scientists screw around so much, I knew I should have gotten a mechanic to take me."

Tara walked quickly back to the spot, scanning the area for him. Petrified logs, pebbles, and another hollow to the left of the sloping rocks filled her view.

"Where are you? Quit lying down, we have a lot of ground to cover." Her voice vibrated with anger.

When she arrived back at the spot, she saw an oxygen mask lying on the ground, without its owner. Pink and orange slime ran under the loose pebbles, and then slid quickly out of sight.

"What the…?"

She scanned the ground for any sign of him, seeing nothing but more pebbles.

"Hey! Hey, where are you?"

Tara pulled off her goggles and squinted against the blinding sunlight.

The blades of another helicopter thudded in the distance.

She scanned to and fro. Nothing. Frozen in indecision she stood for a moment, feeling the blazing sun beat on her face. Turn back? Finish the job? Keep searching for the scientist? After she broke her reverie she noticed movement out of the corner of her eye. Turning toward it, she saw more of the pink and orange slime moving toward her, slowly but deliberately.

Instinct grabbed her, and she turned and ran for her helicopter, only to stop when she saw the pool of pink slime oozing toward her.

She turned to her left and sprinted, trying to flank the gelatinous mass and head back to the helicopter. Spinning to the left, her head kept turning into the spin. She lost her footing and slammed onto the peach rock.

Movement. Animal. Bipedal.

She heard a voice in her mind, akin to remembering a dream.

Her eyes flashed open, staring into the azure dome overhead. She pulled herself to her feet and stumbled forward, breathing heavily behind the oxygen mask.

Oxygen. Homeothermic.

"Who's there?!" She yelled into the air.

Speech.

Turning to the left again, she hopped another log, then stopped dead, facing into another hollow. Its smooth walls slopped gently down. Green and black slime filled this one. It undulated and pulsed as she moved.

Here.

Tara stopped moving, and it stopped moving with her. Her eyebrows furrowed and she squinted hard. Her ears rang.

Yes, it is me. She heard in her mind. Not a clear voice, more of an echo. A memory of someone speaking. It sounded male, like the scientist. She stared at the mass, trying to discern how it was speaking to her.

Questions. You have many.

From the corner of her eye, Tara saw the pink slime stop its advance. It moved back and forth as if waiting for her to move.

Do not worry about them, they are mindless animals. Easy to control. It said, then paused.

I am the one you have to worry about.

"What are you?" Tara demanded, shaking, her eyes wide.

I am what I am. I have always been like this. I always will be.

"What do you want?" She inquired again, her anxiety audible.

To leave this hollow of course. I have been here since the ice covered me so long ago. Thank you for freeing me.

"I didn't free you. Did you kill him?"

Do you mean the person whose name you cannot remember? No. I did not. The animals did. You did free me however, I can read from your mind your species is responsible. You melted the ice. Again, thank you. Now take me away from here.

"No." Tara declared steadfastly, planting both her feet. "I'm betting you can't go far on your own."

You are correct. I cannot, but you can.

"I'm not taking you."

You will do whatever I wish.

Tara felt her arms moving toward the slime and her feet flexed in their boots to move her forward. "No!" She screamed, and threw herself onto the ground, wrapping her arms around a petrified log. "I won't let you get off the mesa. I won't take you with me."

You have no choice. I have moved animals hundreds of times your size. Dinosaurs, reptiles, fish. Powerful things with simple minds. You will not be able to fight me forever.

"I can't take you out if I can't walk."

In a flash, Tara tucked both her legs under a petrified log, and with a quick motion, spun her body around on the hard stone, dislocating both knees. She howled in pain.

That was foolish. You will only delay the inevitable and prolong your suffering.

Through the pain, Tara looked away from the slime and back toward the north, confident she would not allow this creature to get loose.

"Hello?" yelled Lieutenant Ramirez as he jumped out of the helicopter. They landed close enough to Tara to see her get off the ground and limp toward them.

"You are trespassing in the Sector Antártico Argentino and have not been invited. Please leave at once." Ramirez commanded, holding his rifle along his side. He'd never shot anyone while defending their territory before, and he wasn't about to start now. Especially an injured woman. Four other soldiers stepped out of the helicopter, none of them armed.

"I'm sorry," Tara said, her voice raspy and flat, "I took a wrong turn. Got stuck up here during the storm."

She shuffled toward them, moving faster with each step.

"Señora, do you require assistance?" Ramirez inquired. He wore no oxygen mask, and his lips were turning a light blue. Tara's were as brown as ever.

"No. Thank you." She responded, walking past the Lieutenant and not breaking her stride.

"We will… stay here until you leave." Ramirez watched her leave, his head turning to the side as if he couldn't place something.

As Tara approached the last soldier, he met her eyes and nodded slightly.

"Hola," he commented, a chipper upturn in his voice.

Tara said nothing, her face and body pointed toward the north in the direction of her helicopter. Her eyes, however, locked onto his and widened as far as they could, nearly bulging in their sockets. The soldier withered under the gaze and quickly turned to the lieutenant.

Without speaking a word Ramirez gestured to his men to search the area.

Tara, no longer limping but running, quickly reached her helicopter and jumped into the pilot's seat. Without looking at the controls, she turned on all the systems and started the rotors. Her eyes were fixed on the American flag, which fell over the instant the rotor wash hit them.

As the helicopter lifted from the mesa, the sounds of screaming and gunfire filled the air between the thumping of the rotor blades. Tara turned her head as the helicopter banked away, a single tear running down from her left eye.

New Jersey, 2153

It's cold today. The kind of cold that reminds you what winter is actually like. Not the kind of winter we usually get, the colder than autumn. This is gloves and hat weather, even for me. The older I get the more I don't like the cold, but the more I appreciate it.

Yet it wasn't winter. As a matter of fact, it was July. July 16, 2153. 100 years since the North Atlantic conveyor stopped. All heat transfer in the northern hemisphere ground to a slow halt. At first, it wasn't a big deal. Climate change made the summers so hot, and the winters so mild no one minded it not regularly getting to 100 degrees in April anymore. It was nice to have spring actually be spring again. Slowly though, that began to change, and by 2098, the "year without a summer" we understood what was happening. Despite carbon dioxide hitting 470ppm, spring barely woke up from winter. A freak snowstorm hit New York City in June. The snowpack did not recede from the land. Then it all changed.

Crops, at least in Europe and Eastern North America, started failing and it pushed society over the edge. It's amazing that a little bit of adversity caused worldwide panic and dozens of regional conflicts, still with no resolution. Of course, the industrialized nations did well, they had the money and resources to get a stranglehold on the productive areas of the planet. Also, the labor came from millions of displaced persons in the developing world. A new order of sorts had arisen, the way someone accepts the realization that they screwed up, and no amount of cajoling or blaming someone else was going to change it. It was their world now, and the ones who would survive had to be the ones who knew how to exploit it best. The largest irony of the new century: the "Panic of 2100" actually led to the first reduction of atmospheric CO2 since records had been kept. It fell to 470 and has been on a decline ever since.

Eventually, the earth will right itself, and it will be back to normal, but by then no one will be alive who remembers it any other way.

So here I am. It's July. New Jersey. I'm on the beach freezing my ass off. Of course, I ignored all of my friends and didn't move to Florida. It was still getting hammered by hurricanes at least once a month. All thirty million moved to the spine of the state. It was like New York City with palm trees. The state hit the hardest by climate change took it in stride. They did what all Floridians do: ignored it, went to the beach when it wasn't raining, and hoped a sinkhole didn't open under their high rise. There is something to be said about that kind of blasé determination. Just another day in paradise.
I'd rather be cold.

Four Friends Walk into a Bar...

You may not completely understand what happened. Ask a hundred people a question and you get a hundred answers, right? I'm the only person who knows exactly how it happened though because I watched the whole thing, the whole time. My name is Chris Kay.

This punk band from New Jersey got up on stage. "Jungle Punk and the Primes." They were a speed/thrash/screamo standard four-piece. The usual soundcheck kind of band. The audience didn't notice them. I did though, and they screamed amateur. The lead was too self-conscious, the drummer too technical and didn't know how to rest to let the others catch up. The lead guitar, the singular professional in the whole outfit, exuded precision and timing. Expert work on the frets, flawless. She knew how to rock. The bass player? He sucked, obviously there for the pickup gig.

They were on their third song of the set when the guy, who I'd been watching the whole time, came up to the stage — right in front of the audience — grabbed the mic stand and started beating the lead. No one helped him. Up on the balcony, I couldn't get down in time. Security threw the house lights on, and I got forced out. I took a last view of the stage and saw his body, still twitching, sprawled out on the stage. The band, strangely, laughed at him and pointed. How cruel! They were accessories to murder!

To whom it may concern, my name is Skylar Jay, and I was asked by the restaurant association to write this letter based on what I witnessed at the Lakeland Club on the night of June 17, 2024. I came to the club with my friends, to whom you have spoken, and who have given statements. Club security required me to write you this letter before I left the premises.

I stood at the bar, acquiring libations for my friends, Chris Kay, Kim Em, and Pat Bees. Chris sat up in the balcony, taking in the crowd as they are wont to do. Kim hung out on the floor talking to the sound engineer, with whom they had an established rapport.

Pat stood out of my line of sight, so I could not ascertain their whereabouts at the time of the incident.

The bar was congested with patrons, making it difficult to hear the waitstaff. I do not completely recollect the name of the band, as I briefly scanned the marquee of the club upon entering the establishment. "Bunk and the Bunkmates" I believe. I can presume it was near the middle of the opening set when the music suddenly stopped. I am not a fan of this particular type of music. I believe it is called 'House'. I attended that evening because my aforementioned friends wanted an evening out.

Given the opportunity of the quiet, I asked the barkeep for our orders. He stared past my position in the direction of the stage. When I turned to see the commotion, I realized the sound had not stopped because the set ended, but rather because the lead singer left the stage and engaged in a physical altercation with an audience member. Their argument was heated and laced with expletives.

After a brief scuffle, club security swarmed the audience member. Presently, the lead hoisted himself back up onto the stage and subsequently collapsed over his microphone stand. He fell to the stage in a heap and I could see from his expression he was having a difficult time breathing, and his face contorted with pain.

The house lights came on, and I was ordered out of the club. I made a mental note to attend to the well-being of my friends as quickly as possible once we were reunited. I am probably mistaken, however, I thought I heard the sound of laughter coming from the stage.

That is all I am able to recall at the moment. Please contact me for any clarifications.

Skyler Jay

@skylerjay2020

"Hi, Kim!" Bob the engineer shouts at me over the set. Whoever these guys are, they are pretty good. Kids, but they have talent. I think they need exposure. Drummer kicks!

"Heeey Bob!" I belt back at him. He's cool. Tells me a lot of what's going on. "What's shakin'?"

Bob nods at me, he's got a crazy smile. Something is up. "So glad you made it in time!"

"What's up?" Bob can never just come out with it. But he's cool. I will put up with him like I always do.

Man, she shredded that G.

A drunk dude yells "You Suck!"

The guitarist flips him off. She's got cool black nail polish on. Going with the whole goth/death-metal look. She didn't miss getting back on the neck. Props.

"Who are these guys?" I yell at Bob.

"Jungle Funk and the Playmates." He says and shakes his head 'whatever'. He doesn't know shit. He forgets all of them.

"They are pulling a viral something with the band getting killed onstage or whatever."

"Wha? That's messed up." I can dig. Everyone is trying to be the next big TikTok star.

I spin my head around Skylar is at the bar buying us the booze. Chris is up in the balcony. Favorite seat as usual, eh? Typical. Where is Pat? Sigh.

"Here it comes!" Bob yells, excitedly.

This dude, pretty big, is walking toward the stage. I thought he was a bouncer. He starts yelling up to the lead.

I can't hear it over the music. The band is playing louder. Guess it's on purpose.

OMG! They are horrible actors. The lead raises his fists. The band stops. He jumps off the stage. The dude catches him. Wow. Impressive. Quick back and forth. Soft punches. Giggling? They are giggling. Dude, make it look real at least. Sigh.

Here come the bouncers. Ha! That's funny!

The lights come on and the lead jumps back on stage. LOL fell over the mic. He's laughing.

What? The house lights? Whiskey Tango Foxtrot!

"Yeah, I'm going!" I yell at security cuz I'm sauntering out. I glance back at Bob. He's laughing. I'm gonna punch him when they let us back in.

The band finds this really funny. They all have their phones out. The security does too. Yeah, funny guys. If I don't get back in, I'm getting my money back.

Chris and Skylar are already outside. There is Pat! On the phone.

"Hey, yeah it's Pat. I dunno I left the club to get some air. Too tight in there. I dunno. I'm sure I'll get three different stories. Yeah. Kim is the only one who knows what's up, ever. Everyone else is clueless. Yeah, I see them."

Pat speaks into the cellphone. Finger in the opposite ear to block out the noise of the crowd exiting the Lakeland Club.

"What? Some Jersey band… yeah. 'Jungle Hunk and the Primates'… yeah. I dunno. You did? You have? Ha! Whatever. Ok, I'll call you back."

"What happened?!"

Look at Me When I'm Talking to You

"Bryan!" called a woman's voice from the kitchen.

Bryan sat in his living room, headphones strapped on as he played Minecraft on his laptop.

She called again "Bryan!"

Somewhere in the recesses of his mind, he heard a buzzing sound. The same sound he often heard when his mom tried to get his attention, while he was checked out as usual.

Finally, Christmas break arrived, and Bryan returned home from East Tennessee University. Completely content to do nothing in the three weeks he had off between semesters, he brought nothing with him save his dirty laundry. His mother, of course, would have other ideas.

"BRYAN!"

He reached up and took his headphones off. He heard nothing.

Before he could put the headphones back on, a warm hand grabbed his and he stopped.

"Yes, that was me."

Slowly he glanced up at his mother while she stared down at him with the "I'm not mad, just disappointed" expression.

"Yes, mom?" He said, not being snarky.

"Garbage. You. Out now." she said perfunctorily.

"Me Tarzan, you Jane." He said as he got up from the floor and walked into the kitchen. For that, he received a smack on the rump.

Minutes later he tossed the bag of garbage into the can at the end of the driveway.

It had been snowing consistently for the last few hours. Bryan wondered how long he could avoid shoveling before she solicited his help with that too.

He scanned up the street at the other houses. They were festooned with all manner of decorations. The neighborhood always delighted in a friendly competition, and this year, it reached a new level of absurdity.

Bryan liked the silliness but also hated the amount of effort put into such a frivolous task.

He came back in and kicked off his boots. His own house had modest decorations. His mother, always a traditionalist, did not go overboard.

Bryan sat back down on the floor with his back to the tree. He positioned himself so he could see his mother in the kitchen, lest she surprise him again. He put his headphones on again and picked up where he left off.

His mother cooked, and he played. Slowly, the buzzing returned and he shot a glance at his mother. She read from her latest book while waiting for the oven to finish cooking the arroz con pollo she transferred from the stovetop.

"Mom?" He called up. "Did you need me?"

She looked up from the book and shook her head no.

Bryan shrugged and went back to playing. The buzzing returned.

"No Bryan, I'm not talking. Take those off, you're hearing things." She said, gesturing toward the headphones.

Bryan took the headphones off and put them on the table. He kept his mother in eyeshot and went back to the game.

Buzz. Bryan glanced up, first at his mother. Then the door. Then out of the window past the Christmas tree. Nothing.

He shook his head and went back to the game.

Minutes later, buzzing again.

He whipped his head around. Nothing. Except, the branch behind him wasn't where he remembered it.

He adjusted the ornaments and sat on the couch this time. Staring straight at the tree.

Buzzing again.

He could have sworn the branch just moved.

He rubbed his eyes. He'd been playing too long.

Buzzing. Another branch.

He leaned forward, not believing his eyes. The branches were moving! He leaned in closer, a branch articulated like it was being remote-controlled. First at the tip, then down the branch.

"What the...?"

In a flash, all the branches flew toward his face, and everything went dark.

"BRYAN!"

The Outquisition of Reston

"The pods aren't moving that fast, do they look slow to you?"

Richard glanced at the slowly growing green mass as it enveloped the rusting hulk of twisted metal in front of him.

"What are you talking about?"

Richard called to the coordinator, barely glancing up from his display. His coordinator came over and surveyed the situation. "They seemed to be moving faster when we left South Lakes, didn't they?"

"How fast do you want them to go? It's digesting that..." Richard tried to see under the tendrils of the nano-foam pod as it slowly snaked over the metal, "...I think it's a truck."

Richard looked at the green line of cabling, resembling a tree branch, snaking away from the truck, over the parking lot, and into the distance to the east. The branch eventually connected with a massive construct: The Trunk. A combined living space, transport, and self-replicating nano-foam conduit; the Trunk stretched down route 267 toward Washington, D.C. Bulbous pods grew and shrunk along it in response to the amount of new materials being added into the system. Eventually, everything drained into the center of the city, leaving the countryside clean and devoid of human detritus. The Trunk rolled gently over the landscape in the old roadbed, green and white, absorbing sunlight, incorporating new materials, and providing housing for residents of the area who had grown tired of living in the ruins of the old world.

The crew of "Outquisition Wayfarers" just arrived at this location, still called Reston even though it bore no resemblance at all to the former placename and were attempting to recycle it into the Trunk. The main built-up part of The City terminated at Tyson's Corner, and from there the Trunk spread along the old highways of 267, 66, 50, and 395. Beyond that everything was slowly being reverted to forest.

Finally, the tendrils enveloped the last vestiges of the truck, and a new pod began to form. When it finished growing, all the parts in the ancient machine would be reconstituted into new materials and then sent down the stem to the Trunk. Richard analyzed the pod with the scanners in his eyepiece; he didn't even waste time and jumped right into the infrared.

"Let's see," he said softly as his coordinator walked off. "Bets this time?" Richard called out before the coordinator made it out of earshot.

"Eh? Four," he said dismissively as a robotic transport pulled into the old parking lot. It stopped and announced its presence by beeping, flashing, and rhythmically vibrating the ground.

The tendrils separated where they contacted the ground. Four squirrels darted from the opening, scampering toward the brush behind Richard.

"Four," Richard sighed with slight exasperation.

"Lucky guess," his coordinator called back as he poured over the contents of the foundry in the back of the transport. This site had more raw materials and pollutants than was usual along the line, and the Trunk called for the foundry.

The coordinator, Ronnie, set the foundry onto the hood of a decaying Tesla. The batteries had already been removed, and the aluminum frame would be repurposed to haul materials that did not need to be broken down on the molecular level. Right now, it served as a frame for the foundry to start creating the pieces to set up the camp for the evening.

"We're staying?" Richard asked as the slow stream of parts emerged from the back of the foundry: sheets of flexible carbon fiber were the first to emerge, next would-be carbon tube frames, and then finally protein packs.

Ronnie took a drink from his water bottle and glanced up at the sky, the sun shone brilliantly in its azure dome.

"Yeah, I don't think we can clear all this out by sunset." He looked at the foundry that connected directly into a pod in the process of digesting a large truck. " Well, at least it doesn't think we can."

"I'll let her know," Richard said, with a sigh.

Ronnie turned back to the foundry and stacked a sheet of fiber on the ground next to the frame of the old Model X.

"Not like you have anywhere you need to be, right?" he asked, without really needing or wanting an answer.

Richard laughed and glancing down at his dusty boots, then back up to the terminus of the Trunk in the distance, torn between the desire to finish the job out here and a soft, warm bed back home.

"Wayfarer's life for me," he turned and walked past the pods toward the back of the parking lot.

Plopping down in a tree-shaded spot next to the communications array, he took out his bottle of water.

"Hey," he said after taking a swig, "we're staying here tonight. Better make sure we have redundancy set up."

The comm officer, Amanda, looked up from the screen of her bamboo laptop as if she were surprised to hear someone speaking to her.

"Amanda, hello?" Richard said, staring into her in the eyes and waving his hand. The eye not hidden behind a screen focused directly on him, then narrowed. Not breaking her gaze, she tapped a quick sequence on her keyboard and hit enter with particular emphasis.

"I heard you, jerk," a synthetic female voice spoke back to him. Amanda added even more emphasis by sticking her tongue out, trying to repress a smile at the same time.

"You're a funny woman," Richard responded.

She nodded at him with a flourish of her right hand, the LED comm band on it flashing wildly.

"Can I get you anything?" he asked, rummaging through his pack searching for a protein bar. Everything had been packed so tightly one false pull and the contents would instantly go out of order. That already happened hours ago, and now the similarly packed contents were a jumble of cardboard boxes, thankfully color-coded.

"Strawberry?" came from Amanda's comm band.

Richard fished around in his pack, finally, on the bottom, lay a strawberry protein pack. With a quick smile, he tossed the pack over to Amanda, who caught it with a wild billow of her orange and purple afro.

She shook her head and signed "laughter" in American Sign Language, with her free hand, which she then inverted to her middle finger. Richard could see her back shaking as she turned away; staccato breaths escaping her mouth.

Moments later, Ronnie came by the camp with his water and protein and sat down under the tree.

"Amanda, why are you in the sun?" he asked her. The heat had already gotten unbearable for the September afternoon.

Amanda responded by pointing at the communications array, and then up at the sky.

Ronnie gazed over at Richard and raised his eyebrows. She was in her zone and it would be a waste of time, not to mention insulting, to suggest she leave it.

Scanning back over to the foundry, Ronnie could see the transport bot had shifted to its humanoid form and started assembling the carbon tube frame. Next to the frame lay impeccably stacked carbon fiber sheets. Impregnated with solar, the carbon fiber sheets would only needed to be snapped together to start providing power.

Richard scanned across the parking lot to the buildings behind; another office park, separated from everything by an access road. On and on they stretched along 267. One leap-frogged development after another. He shook his head in disbelief.

"Yeah I know," Ronnie said looking in the same direction and running his hands through his jet-black hair, "I wonder how they felt when they realized everything was a house of cards?"

Richard grunted softly to himself.

"How long do you want to stay? Since we are setting up camp anyway?" Richard asked.

"We could be here as long as we want — remember that time in Centerville?"

Richard thought back to the time they helped outquisition the exurb. It took nearly two months, and they were only one of seventeen teams crawling across the hectares of low-density development. Murderous heat and humidity; teams fought rampant heatstroke, even with all the precautions. Medical Nomad teams — Medmads — flooded the area for weeks. In the end, the entire area rewound to the Trunk, providing the material for housing ten thousand people downtown.

"Medmads are setting up facilities nearby," Ronnie added.

"Why don't we take one building at a time?" Richard offered.

Ronnie chuckled and took another sip of water.

"Okay, let her decide. Amanda?" Richard called her way, "Which one?"

Amanda keyed a few commands into her laptop and then closed it. She stood up slowly, arched her back, and then took a deep breath. She stared at the buildings for several minutes, occasionally swatting mosquitoes. Still, she refused to get out of the sun.

She pointed to the tallest building, behind the one directly in front of the parking lot. Richard felt his heart sink.

"Told ya," Ronnie chortled.

Richard shook his head, both out of exasperation and respect for the comm officer. "She's hardcore."

The team spent the night under the carbon fiber shelter constructed for them, the beds grown on the spot from composite materials made by the nano-foam. Richard took pride in the fact his comforter and pillow were nearly indistinguishable from the 'natural' bamboo ones in his apartment. Not that he used it — still too warm during the evenings — and he longed to return home to his climate-controlled apartment in The Trunk. As much as he thought it important to rewind the detritus from the "Century of Excess," he'd been a Wayfarer for the last seven months and needed a break.

When they woke, a brilliant new Personal glistened alongside the shelter, compliments of the foundry and the transport bot. Running water, a warm shower, and a toilet that wasn't nano-foam in a bucket. Amanda had already been using it when Richard finally swung his legs out of bed. Ronnie, reading an update on stockpiles, nodded his head.

"Mornin'," Richard croaked.

"Glad you could join us," Ronnie quipped. "You're next to hit the Personal. There is some fresh protein at the foundry."

"Where's the coffee?" Richard searched around smiling, taking a deep breath of air.

The door of the Personal popped open, and Amanda stepped out, her hair pulled back into a puffy ponytail. She grinned and pointed to the table next to her bed; a pot of coffee simmered contentedly.

From Amanda's comm band, "It's about time, sleepyhead. I've already had two cups."

Nothing like getting ribbed by a synthesized voice first thing in the morning, Richard thought to himself.

"Are we getting to work or what?" Amanda's comm chimed in. Its wearer already geared up for the day. Richard didn't even realize she had taken the mesh network down.

Without speaking, Richard grabbed some clothes from his pack and headed into the Personal. Being only slightly bigger than a square meter, the space did not have much room to move around. The toilet, sink, and shower were all in the same space, so it could be completely cleaned and sterilized between each use. Antiseptic and UV light would kill anything without a fairly strong outer skin; even nanites would disintegrate under the onslaught. He stripped naked and threw his clothes into a protected cabinet inside the doorway. Looking into the full-length mirror, he grimaced a bit at the sight of his battered body. Scarred all over from a few decades of wear and tear outquisitioning old cities. Medmads patched him up whenever he needed it. Everything worked fine and the scars were cosmetic, but it still hurt, no matter how good the repair. The grey hair and wrinkles were par for the course. He showered, savoring the warm soapy water and the patter on the back of his neck. He felt a little more human.

He dressed and stepped out of the Personal. The door locked behind him as it started its cleaning procedure. It used more energy than anyone liked, but no one wanted to risk yet another pandemic.

Ronnie came up to him with a protein bar and his canteen.

"She's already in there setting up the mesh for the nanites," he said matter-of-factly.

Richard looked up at the office building and saw the comm array sticking out of one of the broken windows.

"Ronnie, I'm not set yet, she could get hurt," Richard said reproachfully.

"You think I don't know that?" he replied quickly, "I coordinate you guys, but I'm not her boss."

Richard sighed and walked quickly to his bunk to get his comm band. He needed to direct the nano-foam toward the building. Once they were in range of the array, the nanites would self-organize and pick the building apart from the top down.

Lifting his comm band to his face, he called to the comm officer, "Not a race, Amanda!"

The computer voice responded, "You never left the starting line."

Richard shook his head and started off to the office building. He admired her tenacity and drive, but his experience told him she took too many risks and one day…

He never got to finish his thought before the building started rumbling.

"Amanda!" He yelled into his comm band, as he watched dust and debris fly out of the windows. The floors collapsed in sequence, starting with the top and pancaking down. He flung himself against the side of the closest building and threw his hands over his head. He heard the slamming metal sound of the transport bot running toward the collapsing structure. It would not stop, no matter the risk to itself.

For what felt like an eternity, he listened to the sickening sound of exploding brick and concrete and he felt the rumble of the impacts through the ground. He'd seen a few building collapses in his career, both intentional and accidental, but never one with someone inside it.

When the rumbling stopped, he surveyed the dust-choked sky, a hundred years of decay flying all around him, mixed with who knows what toxic chemicals used to make the building "safe."

"AMANDA! ARE YOU OKAY?" Richard yelled into the air, running at top speed toward the rubble that used to be a ten-story building.

"AMANDA!" Ronnie yelled over and over, with no response.

Richard grabbed a pod that was deconstructing a small car and carried it over to the rubble pile. It squirmed in protest, trying to latch its tendrils back onto whatever inorganic matter it could find.

"Stop fighting me!" he yelled at it. "I need you!"

The pod stopped struggling and went quiescent in his arms. He knew it was not responding to his command, but it's subroutine secured pods for transport. Raw nano-foam, on the other hand, would still be fighting him for stability.

Richard tested the debris for a stable spot to set the pod down. Satisfied, he flipped it onto its side, exposing the tendrils and nano-foam along the base. The tendrils immediately writhed for purchase as it tried to right itself.

"Stay there!" He roared, while frantically keying commands on his comm band.

Within moments, the pod began dissolving, taking all the mass it acquired from the car and converting it back into foam filled with nanites.

The transport bot already began lifting chunks of rubble off the pile. It stacked the pieces as neatly as it could to prevent them from falling again, but not fast enough to free the trapped human from inside. It visibly shook as its potentials to free Amanda, and to avoid hurting her further in the attempt, collided.
Ronnie kept calling on his comm band, hoping for a response. Amanda's transponder continued to signal, but with all the broken steel in the rubble, its exact location could not be fixed. Her heart rate displayed as a pulsating green dot.

"Hurry," he said to Richard, more as a status than a command.

Richard nodded and in one swift move, picked up a handful of nano-foam and threw it into the biggest hole he could find. With a splat, the green mass instantly stuck to the surfaces inside the hole. Within moments, tendrils formed and began snaking through the crevices. He zoomed out on his comm band to watch them filter through the pile. Ronnie briefly glanced at the screen then ran to the transport bot.

"You need to find the nearest Medmads. Now."

A computerized voice spoke back from the transport, a singular green eye, unblinking, "Ms. Amanda possesses the mesh uplink. I do not have the range to seek them out from this location." Its body quivered from the anxiety. "I cannot leave her."

Ronnie shook his head in the affirmative, "I know, get to the Trunk and link from there. She could still die without medical treatment. You're more helpful this way. Hurry."

In less than a second, the transport robot flung itself to the ground and deployed its all-terrain tires. It sped off toward the Trunk at breakneck speed — far faster than it should safely go. With one human hurt and direct command from another, its own safety was its last priority.

"It's on its way!" Ronnie yelled back to Richard as he ran over to the pile again, pulling rubble off as fast as he could.

Richard nodded, eyes focused on the comm band as green lines snaked through the translucent rubble pile, increasing their length every second. Soon the tendrils would find her, and they would begin to dissolve the building.

Richard shook his head in frustration; he wanted to grab rubble and tear it off too, but he was guiding the nano-foam and needed to focus on it. So many times he had been in these situations, helpless and waiting on machines to fix the problem. Problems created by humans centuries ago.

In front of the pair, the hole opened slowly, increasing in diameter every few seconds. Ronnie kept leaning in, trying to see into the dark expanse.

"I can't see," he hurriedly choked out.

"Right," Richard answered and punched in another few commands. The hole slowly filled with pulsing green light, growing in intensity as the hole grew bigger.

"Come on, come on…" Richard whispered anxiously as the tendrils snaked almost into the middle of the pile.

"Outquisition Wayfarers, this is Merry Medmads, come in, over," called a calm male voice from Ronnie's band. The two jumped at the sound of another human.

"Merry Medmads, this is Outquisition Wayfarers, we read you, over," replied Ronnie, desperately trying not to scream into the band.

"What's your status? Over," The Medmad asked.

"A building collapsed with our comm officer inside, she has the mesh uplink. We're receiving her bio-signs, nano-foam is en route. Did the transport bot contact you? Over."

"Affirmative, it's heading back from the Trunk with a new mesh. We're in Herndon, ETA fifteen minutes to your position. Over."

Ronnie turned his head from the band and sighed. Another eternity to wait. "Sounds good. We have no idea of her condition. Please hurry. Over."

"Will do, hang tight. Medmads, out."

"GOT HER!" Richard yelled ecstatically and gesturing wildly to his band for Ronnie to see. Her transponder switched to a solid blue dot, and the tendril similarly switched from green to blue. The other tendrils immediately stopped progressing in other directions and began to converge on her position.

"How long do you think?" Ronnie asked over his shoulder.

"Dunno," Richard shook his head, his grey hairs bouncing around his eyes. "They aren't great at extraction. Let's hope it doesn't make it worse."

Ronnie nodded and turned back to the ever-widening tunnel. "Amanda!" he yelled, "We're coming! Hold on!"

Another update on Richard comm band, and Amanda's status came pouring in. Heart rate at seventy beats per minute and stable. Blood-pressure one hundred over sixty. Oxygen saturation at ninety-seven percent. Neural activity and muscle conductivity were offline.

"She's out cold," Richard said, looking up at the tunnel. "We can stop yelling."

Richard felt the adrenaline ebb from his body, and all his joints complained in unison. He walked over to a large chunk of concrete and sat down with a grunt.

"Ronnie, get some water. Don't pass out on me." Richard attempted to have the coordinator focus on something else for a moment to clear his head. Ronnie stood there, staring at the tunnel. Frustrated, Richard picked up a pebble and hurled it at his leg. "RON!"

Ronnie pulled his attention away from the tunnel, as though he'd heard a loud sound in the distance. He shook his head and walked back to the Personal.

The transport bot swung around the side of the portable bathroom. In an instant, it stood up from its horizontal position, tucked back its all-terrain wheels, and ran toward Richard. A new mesh network uplink cradled in its bulky hands.

Richard stood up and waved it over.

"Go," Richard intoned as he took the uplink from the bot, and without missing a step it ducked into the tunnel.

Ronnie came back with a bottle of water for Richard, and almost followed the bot into the tunnel.

"Don't do that, there will be two of you stuck in there," Richard admonished while he pointed the antenna of the uplink toward the Trunk.

He looked back at his comm band; the pulsing green light of the transport bot flashed halfway between the opening and Amanda's location. Before it, a mass of green and blue tendrils slowly increased the tunnel diameter.

"Okay, let's see what the world has been up to," Richard joked as he keyed in the connection sequence to the uplink. In a wave of data, their comm bands sprang into life. Instantly connecting them to the rest of the Trunk, to The City, and ultimately to the rest of the world.

"Merry Medmads to Outquisition Wayfarers, come in, over," The male voice returned.

"Wayfarers here, go ahead Medmads, over," Ronnie spoke into his band.

"Received your comm officer's vitals, ETA one minute, prepare to receive, out."

"Copy, we're ready, out."

"When this is over," Richard breathed, "I think I'm done."

Ronnie stared at the veteran nano-engineer, "Why?"

"I've been in the sun too long," Richard pointed up to his sunburned, wrinkled face.

Ronnie smiled and nodded. They stared at the tunnel for a minute. It was an uncomfortable silence, but also one of acceptance of an axiom.

"Hey there! How is she?" Called the male voice of the medmad comm officer from behind the rubble, in the other direction of the parking lot.

The pair looked around the debris to see several people in powered white and green exosuits clambering over the rubble. Their long, stilt-like legs propelling them effortlessly.

Richard felt relief wash over him. "Thanks for getting here so fast!" He called to the new arrivals, each of whom contained enough medical equipment to be considered an individual field hospital.

"Our pleasure," another called down from eight feet in the air; Richard could see her brown eyes smiling down at him.

Three of the five medmads dismounted and set up triage equipment. One waited by the entrance to the tunnel, which grew in size quickly now, while their comm officer scanned their bands for other people needing assistance.

Waiting by the tunnel, the medmad who had spoken to Richard earlier called down, "We've got a scan on her…" She read the data stream as it came into her comm band, calling down to the triage area as she assessed, "… broken left femur… broken left wrist… uh some blood loss… concussed… amazing, no ruptured organs… she's aphasic?"

Richard spoke up to her, his eyes squinting against the midday sun, "Yeah, she got really sick as a kid. Brain damage."

"I can see that," she said, analyzing the data, "… we can fix this." She looked quickly down at Richard, asking for permission more than stating a fact. He promptly shook his head in the negative.

"She'd kill all of us," he responded with a wry smile.

She laughed and shook her head, "Just the new stuff guys."

"I have Ms. Amanda. We are coming out. Please prepare." The transport bot's voice broke over all the comm bands on the emergency frequency.

The medmad stepped back from the entrance to the tunnel and retracted the exosuit legs, leaving her at ground level. She put both arms through straps behind her back and pulled the struts from the legs up and onto her arms. As easily as slipping on a backpack, the leg struts became arm braces, tripling her arm strength. Richard smiled at the versatility.

"Amanda! We're here! Hang on!" Ronnie called into the tunnel nervously.

The low profile of the transport bot rolled into view. Amanda, covered in nano-foam, lay on the bed. She snapped back into consciousness when the sunlight hit her face, agony and confusion contorting her blood-streaked cheeks.

"It's okay," the medmad spoke in a soothing voice as she lifted Amanda off the bed. "You were in an accident. Your friends called us. Can you hear me?"

Cradled in the medmad's arms, Amanda shook her head yes and squeezed her eyes against the blinding sun.

"That's good, Amanda," she added trying to assess her mental state. "You're aphasic, is that right?" She lay Amanda on the triage bed, while the others quickly peeled off nano-foam and set up IVs.

Amanda shook her head again yes.

"Your friends say it's safer that way. Is that right?" She added with a smile, attempting to break the tension.

Amanda's chest shook and breaths came in staccato bursts again.

Richard leaned over them and met her eyes. He smiled broadly, his grey hair dangling in front of his face.

Amanda brought her right hand up to her lips, palm facing her — Richard assumed she was about to flash him the finger again — then out toward him. "Thank you," she signed.

"It's okay sweetie. Rest. You'll be fine."

Richard sat up in his bed, and the cool bamboo flooring, soft to the touch, greeted his feet. He looked around his bedroom; wood-framed white plaster walls, bamboo furniture. The window on the far side of the room automatically opened as it sensed him moving. The view overlooked the main transit line of the Trunk; trains and transport pods sliding silently along magnetic tracks.

In the distance, the sprawling buildings of Reston, which were slowly being rewound, baked in the intense sunlight. A single white cloud hung in the hazy azure sky.

Richard walked over to his Personal and splashed water onto his face. He glanced up at his reflection; his grey hair cut short, sunburn gone, salt and pepper beard cropped close against his brown skin. He contemplated the lines on his face, a testament to all the time spent outside saving the world one office park at a time.

"Well, what now?" He said with a grin.

His comm panel went off, indicating a call. He turned around, shirtless, and spoke into the air, "Yes?"

The panel turned on to show the smiling face of Amanda, her dark eyes sparkling, orange and purple afro bouncing playfully.

"Hey, there sweetie! Getting on without me?"

Amanda looked down and typed on her band, it responded, "Hey, old man, yeah we're getting along fine without having to wait on your slow ass." She smiled and squinted her eyes. Behind her, four new wayfarers, and Ronnie, waved to him.

Amanda's band spoke again, "I'm gonna miss you out here. Running around with us. Getting into trouble." A fleeting look of sadness jostled with the wry smile on her face.

"I can't watch your back all the time. Be careful, okay?" He spoke, softly.

"I will." The translator spoke back.

She smiled and signed "thank you" to him.

He signed back and smiled.

The panel shut off, revealing the window out of the other side of the apartment; forest stretched on as far as the eye could see, bright green, and hopeful.

In the Sight of a Bear

3 March 2048

I wear pants. I'd heard all those stories about being the last person on Earth and refusing to wear pants after a while. I think that's a great idea, except when you try it. It's not just the cold. One word: bugs. Holy hell are chiggers and ticks bad. I have nearly a limitless supply of calamine lotion and such, but yeah, I'd rather not have my unmentionables being chewed on. Of course, most of the pants I can find aren't my size. But who's gonna care if I have high waters and ankle socks. I'm pretty good with a needle and thread. Or duct tape, whatever works.

10 March 2048

Wow it's hot today. The thermometer here at the clubhouse registered at 91. There aren't even leaves out yet. I'm not putting my summer crops out. The last frost is still going to nail them and then I'll have no veg for the summer. Screw that. But my lettuce is doing fab!

17 March 2048

Happy St. Patrick's Day!

All the beer went bad a few years back. There is some wine though, but it was never my thing. Potatoes in the ground today. I can't be sure, but I thought there was more white wine in the store. I must have drunk it before I started writing everything down. Went for a swim in the lake. Strange that it's warm, and I can see the bottom. I lived here for what, thirty years and never could see that. Nothing like "The world ending" to fix the world, eh?

11 April 2048

Lit a bonfire. Ran out of candles a few years back.

23 April 2048

Lots of thunder yesterday. The lake started to flood. I think I might need to move up to the summer pavilion sooner this year. Just nuts. Planted my three sisters and all. Hopefully the frost is over. *crossing fingers* I got anxious and pulled some of the spuds. New potatoes. Ahh so nice to have fresh food after the winter eating beans. So many bags of them. I honestly don't know how long they will keep. Seems ridiculous to waste my solar on keeping them frozen.

11 May 2048

39

13 June 2048

Corn is doing well, but I had to plant so much of it because of the deer. Cleaned out my rifle. Prepped the smokehouse.

4 July 2048

Yeah, like that matters anymore. Still, banged rocks together and lit a big bonfire. I have more freedom than any human ever. Woop-dee do. I was up pretty late though, too hot to sleep. Thought I heard something up in the parking lot. Probably a bear. I've been seeing a lot of those lately. Two generations or so have grown up without us. I guess it's not too concerned with the lights in my compound.

6 August 2048

My crops came in! Soooo many! So much food. It was never this good. Like ever. Of course, 90% is gonna rot before I can eat it. But I can't walk away from planting as much as I can.

26 August 2048

Put my second crop into the ground today. I can easily get pumpkins and squash going before the first frost. If it's later, great. I need to take better accounting of my food here. I think there is a bag of beans missing. My phone's camera stopped working and I haven't been able to… liberate another one from one of the neighbors. I'll have to start locking the food away better. I must have left the door unlocked. Bear.

11 September 2048

So, while I investigated a house nearby, I stumbled across a whole video recording system. Petabytes of space. Head-strap camera. Mountain bikes in the garage (rotten wheels though). I buried the bodies as a thank you for giving me their equipment. I ran through what they had stored for a few days. Family, eldest daughter in college. It felt weird hearing new voices again. After a while I realized I had been too intrusive. I backed up their data onto my Mac and deleted the storage on the camera equipment.

21 September 2048

Still insufferably hot, but I wanted to try out the video equipment. Embedding the video:

Camera POV shows head bobbing as the wearer walks through the forest. Green leaves on trees. Quiet. Crunching leaves underfoot. Breathing. Deer enter the frame from the right. Wearer stops. Another deer follows. Then another. The deer keep their distance. Rifle rises. Gunshot. Running toward carcass. The other deer scatter.

"Pretty crazy, eh? They have no fear anymore and there are so many."

The camera shuts off.

My first "confirmed" kill. Not like anyone will ever see it anyway.

26 October 2048

Camera POV walking through forest along a barely discernible overgrown path.

"I managed to find a new pair of hikers at the local BYSA supply store. I thought I'd been through that place a thousand times. I should have just moved in."

The camera tilts down toward feet. Right boot turned to display.

"Breaking them in. They hurt. Not too bad. Haven't had new shoes in… I dunno, 5 years?"

The camera tilts back up. Stops.

"Thought I heard something. The bear are getting really aggressive lately. I think they are carving out new territories without us around anymore. I have to lock down the camp every night. Things are disappearing."

31 October 2048

Happy Halloween! It's a beautiful one today. The sky is so blue. The leaves are barely turning. I've seen worse.

The camera turns on. Pans around the lake from right to left. Dilapidated carousel with clothes hanging from the beams. Small bridge arching over the stream. Open lake. Spillway and dam. Small, covered pavilion with containers filled with water surrounded by various fire pits. Turns back toward the path.

"Gonna hike for a bit. Work can wait."

The camera turns off.

The camera turns on. POV bobbing. Dense forest. Group of deer in the distance. Black bear cub to the right.

"Crap. Don't have my gun."

The camera turns to the left, walking pace quickens.

"I… hope… mama…"

The bear roars in the distance

The camera jerks as head bobs become jumbled. Flashing sky, forest, sky, forest. Sound of feet pounding, breath coming in fast spurts.

"HEY! HEY!"

Tumbling. Grunting. The camera points up at the sky. Leaves obscure part of the lens.

"HEY! WAIT! I… YOU?!"

"STAY BACK!" *A woman's voice screams.*

"OKAY WAIT!" *Man replies.*

"It's OKAY!"

"The bear?!" *The woman asks.*

"I see her. She's back with the cub. It's okay… I'm glad I'm wearing pants!"

The man nervously chuckles, she joins slowly.

The ma picks the camera off the ground, fingers obscure the lens.

"MY CAMERA!" Woman exclaims. "HOW DID YOU…?"

"I'm sorry, our neighborhood… completely deserted. I thought I was the only one… I'm sorry about your family. I buried them in the backyard. I didn't think… you know…"

"I saw. I wondered who was so… caring. They didn't take anything but the camera."

Fingers part from the lens revealing a woman in her 20s. Her hair is pulled back into a ponytail. Baseball cap. Leather jacket. Tears running down her dirty face.

"Sophia, right?"

The camera POV moves back up to the view from his head. He is significantly taller than she. The camera pans down.

"Yeah. Guessed you watched it."

"A little bit, but then I put it away. Backed it up and everything."

Woman smiles.

"We'd better move. She's still around. Daniel by the way."

The man's hand stretches away from the body toward Sophia. Then stops halfway and pulls back.

"Do you… mind?" *She says sheepishly.*

"Of course." *He says quickly.* "It's been a while."

He laughs. They walk toward camp.

The camera turns off.

18 November 2059

Mom said I shouldn't play with dad's old journal. But I can't stop. He had so much in here! He kept all the vids from her house and everything he'd written since he was alone right up until he died. So much stuff!

Imagine what that was like? Before mom came back from Boston. Before I was born. Before we met The Others. They were alone, totally alone. They never were though, things were different.

I love watching the old vids. I can't quite explain the world back then. So many people. So much noise! A lot of anger. It's cool and terrifying at the same time. I couldn't imagine living there though. It must be why they named me after my great grandmother: Hope.

Ember Angel

"Stan, get that roof open!"

The fire chief yelled at the closest fireman to get up onto the roof and break it open. It needed to be ventilated so the fire could breathe properly.

"Yes Chief!"

Stan grabbed his axe and climbed up the ladder propped up against the side of the apartment building.

Flames and thick smoke belched from the second- and third-floor windows of the building; acrid and smothering, the choking fumes were a powder keg waiting to explode.

Jumping up onto the creaking roof, Stan swung his axe over his head, years of training made his swings sure.

One swing. Then two. The asphalt shingles flew in every direction. Swinging a six-pound axe with his Scottie SCBA on his back took strength and stamina, both of which he had. The hardest part of the process was dealing with the fear, by simply ignoring it. That's what training is for.

On the top of the third swing, the peak of the roof gave in, and his right foot plunged into the hole, trapping his leg.

He yelled down to the commander, "Chief!"

The chief nodded and looked across to two other firemen drawing lines from the truck. Without speaking he pointed to them and then up at the roof where Stan waved his arms. They, in turn, yelled to another fireman to finish hooking the lines while they ran to the ladder.

Stan still had the axe in his right hand, as smoke billowed up from the hole that encased his leg. He knew if he pulled at the opening to remove his leg, he could be weakening the structure even further. If his two companions stepped wrong, they could all fall through the roof. The decision wasn't his to make though, and in a moment of creaking and splintering, the roof opened beneath him and he fell through.

He slammed hard onto the floor of what appeared to be an attic. Choked with smoke and ash, he could not see more than a foot in front of his face; worse still, he couldn't breathe. In nine seconds, he got to his knees, masked up, checked the regulator, and started breathing clean air.

Quickly he assessed his body. Nothing hurt. He moved his joints, everything bent without pain.

Grabbing his mic and holding it up to the emitter in his facemask, he keyed the radio to transmit.

"I'm okay!" He yelled into the mic and waited for a response. The air rushing past and the flames below made it nearly impossible to hear. He transmitted again, "I'm okay."

When he looked down at his chest, he could see the cut line from the mic to the radio.

"Damn, the fall."

Shooting a glance back up at the ceiling where he fell through, only a small patch of daylight weakly shone behind the black smoke. He couldn't tell if his crew worked above trying to get to him, or below trying to work the fire. On his own for the moment, he relied on his training and self-confidence.

He scanned around for his axe but could not find it.

"Probably still on the roof." He reassured himself.

The attic comprised a full-sized room that you only see in movies, not a crawl space with a door. Every house in the city had an attic like this, and they were the bane of many a firefighter. Usually filled with a century of bric-a-brac, they would go up like a matchbox in a fully involved fire. Luckily this one had little in it, and it gave him room to maneuver.

Assessing his area, he looked across and found the stairs leading down. Another decision awaited him: to go down and attempt to exit the area — hoping he actually could — or wait inside the location for his crew to find him. He attempted to stay put, as his training told him, and look for the closest safe exit. Again, his decision was made for him.

"HELP! H—HELP!"

A voice cried from beneath him. He tried to localize the scream.

"I'M HERE!" he yelled at the floorboards. "I'm coming!"

Before he could turn, he felt something grab his right arm, and a wave of searing pain shot to his shoulder.

Shifting his weight to his left, he turned to look right, expecting to see a flaming beam or pipework on his arm. He saw nothing there, just more of the acrid smoke.

He yanked his arm back, hoping to break free of something unseen in the black billow, but he could not. He reached with his other hand and firmly grasped his right arm. Nothing held it.

He shifted his weight again and moved toward the stairs. He still could not move, but the pain stopped.

"What the…?"

Black smoke enveloped him, yet he could see clearly enough to make out a figure, taller than he and less substantial; a roughly human form, traced out by swirling eddies of smoke and burning embers.

Quickly he thought out the possibilities and his spine reacted before his mind could grasp the situation. He reached for the figure with his left arm, assuming one of his crew stood there, engulfed in flames. The searing pain tore through his hand and up his arm, and he yanked it back in agony.

Instantly, the pain ceased, almost as if it had never been.

"HELP!" The voice cried from beneath the floorboards.

"I'M COMING!" He yelled into the air while trying to get a good look at the figure; smoke and embers swirled and writhed. Ephemeral yet solid.

The fireman turned back to the stairs — whatever this entity composed itself of, it delayed his progress and interfered with his job. He turned to the stairwell and willed his feet to move as quickly as they could, floorboards creaked with every step.

He felt he could move this time and felt no pain. Not completely understanding what changed, Stan took the opportunity and bolted for the stairs. Instantly the smoke and embers enveloped him, but he pushed forward and ran on instinct. All down the single flight of stairs, he fought the embers, as if it were conscious of his presence; he pushed, shoved, and used his body as leverage against it. He could not shake the feeling that it headed down the stairs as well.

Bounding around the corner, the room greeted Stan in an inferno. The walls were completely engulfed in flames and smoke, broken beams crackled like fireworks all around him. The floor, soaked with water and charcoal, was as slippery as ice. He could barely discern the open windows to his right, their openings meekly glowing against the conflagration around him. Visibility hovered near zero. He knew the air itself filled with hydrocarbons, like vapors from a can of gasoline, waiting to explode once an influx of oxygen gave it enough fuel. The very thing he attempted to stop when he climbed on the roof to ventilate the building.

"PLEASE!" The woman screamed.

"I'M LOOKING FOR YOU!" He yelled as he tried to localize her calls.

Grabbing his flashlight from his belt, Stan scanned the red-stained darkness; its white beam barely cutting in front of him.

You have to find her. He recited over and over in his head. *I'm not losing another one.*

"WHERE ARE YOU?" He called out, sensing the time to act slipping away.

"H — HERE!" *cough* "Here!" The second call came across much weaker. Stan dropped to his knees and slammed through the smoke, barely looking around, aimed right at the last cry.

He scuttled across the floor keeping his hands away from hotspots of flame licking up through the floorboards. A chaos of fire, smoke, and water. One more time he called out:

"WHERE ARE YOU?"

Nothing.

He called again.

Nothing.

He moved forward in the only direction he thought might lead him to her. One last foot and the smoke cleared enough to see the bottom of a door. Smoke billowed away from it as the air from behind was being pulled into the room. He knew if he opened the door he could cause a backdraft and the whole floor could explode. She lay behind that door.

"Shit," He growled through his teeth.

Normally he would advise his crew he planned to open a closed door, but with his mic cut off that proved impossible.

"I'M COMING IN!" He yelled as loud as he could so someone would hopefully hear, then hurled himself at the door.

As quickly as he shot toward it, the embers returned, standing right in his path.

Stopping quickly, Stan traced the shape of the embers, like a person, but more like a cloud. Like the steam coming from a kettle at full boil; smoke, and orange and red embers swirling. At his full height, he could stare right into the head of the figure. It slowly turned toward him, faceless save for a glowing spot where he knew a mouth should be.

"Help…" she gasped from behind the door.

The firefighter's universe constricted to this point. This infinitesimal point in time and space. Everything slowed down and grew quiet, with only the sound of him breathing through his mask filling his ears. He fully realized the true nature of the situation.

"You can't have her," he whispered, peering through the swirling smoke and embers. "Not this time." Then, ignoring his training and not checking the door, he lunged forward with all of his strength and will.

His world flew back into searing reality; a white-hot agony that consumed his entire body. With a scream unlike anything he ever heard before, the door exploded in front of him — flaming wooden shrapnel filled the air. The firefighter held himself steady and waited for his eyes to adjust.

"I'M HERE!" He shouted as he scanned the room as quickly as he could.

He entered the small windowless bedroom adorned with floral patterns and pastels that now peeled from the walls as the room rapidly filled with smoke. Medical equipment lined the far wall, all with no power. To his right, a single hospital-style bed with pink blankets spanned the length of the short wall. Wrapped in those blankets lay an elderly woman, disheveled grey hair falling about her shoulders, oxygen tube right below her nose.

In front of the bed, and carrying the full weight of the woman's gaze, the ember figure stood.

"No!" Stan cried, "NO!"

He tore forward; lunging toward the woman who took absolutely no notice of him; she stared, rather placidly, up at the hulking figure.

The figure reached a tendril of smoke and embers toward the firefighter, without ever moving its 'face' from the woman. With supernatural force, Stan was thrown against the wall of the bedroom. He hit with a sickening crack as it partially collapsed around him. Pinned, and with his mask ripped from his face, Stan reflexively held his breath and tried to break free from the figure's grasp. The overwhelming force pushed him against the wall, and he gasped for air. Within moments, smoke filled his nose and mouth, its super-heated contents being drawn into his lungs. The white-hot agony returned, and his body spasmed violently.

And then, everything stopped.

Time as he understood it froze, white light filled the room, and a complete and utter calm overtook him.

He gazed at the woman, still gazing upward serenely; her face soft and glowing, relaxed, unconcerned with anything in the world.

He looked at the figure, now sharply defined. The swirling smoke and embers tightly constrained against some unseen surface. It writhed and bubbled like the contents of an orange lava lamp. He could see clearly now, the figure had two legs without feet, their trunks meeting the floor but showing no signs of weight or compression. Six arms extended out from the sides of the figure, distributed evenly across the space. They had no hands and no obvious signs of joints. Mere tubes of smoke, one of which held Stan to his spot. A short neck held the head, which bore no earthly face. It glowed with a sharp and defined orange light.

"I have to save her," Stan pleaded to the figure. "She needs me."

He felt a tug at his pants and looked down.

There, splayed at his feet, lay the body of his crew-mate who died three years previously. Helmet off, soot staining his face and nostrils. His ear and half his face burned away.

"Miguel…" he choked out his name.

"Is she ok?" Miguel looked up, trying to focus on him through swollen shut eyes.

"The little girl? She's fine. You saved her." Tears welled in Stan's eyes. Miguel shook his head, satisfied with the outcome. "Told you…" he coughed.

"Relax, the EMTs are coming," Stan said, choking back sobs, tears streaming down his face.

The body disappeared, leaving Stan holding nothing.

He glared back at the figure.

"He saved her; he did his job! You won't let me!" Anger welled within him.

From his left, a small voice called to him. "Daddy? Is Star going to be alright?"

Stan looked down at the small girl, her cheeks streaked with tears. She held a small orange and white hamster in her tiny hands. It had a patch of orange fur around its left eye, roughly in the shape of a star.

"Well," the firefighter said, bending down on one knee to talk to her at her eye level. "Star was just old, sweetie. Hamsters don't live that long."

He looked up to see his backyard on that cool October day. Orange and red leaves gently alighted on the ground; the fire pit crackled happily.

"But, he can't die… he can't… he'll…"

"Never come back," Stan said, reciting the words he will never forget.

"Why?!" she half-sobbed, half-shouted.

"Things die, sweetie when it's time it's time. There is nothing we can do."

"You save people! You can do it!" she said, and he knew that she strained logic to breaking, even for a five-year-old.

"I can't sweetheart."

"I HATE YOU!" She yelled, clutching the lifeless body, and running to the back of the yard, past the fire.

As before, Stan stood in the room, holding nothing.

Again, he glared up at the figure, "That is a hamster, a pet! It's not the same! It was just old." As soon as the words left his mouth, he felt the truth of the statement.

Stan looked at the woman, still frozen in time.

From his left, Stan heard a beeping sound. He turned and walked toward the hospital bed that appeared in front of him. The windows in the room were open wide, sunlight pouring in. The small flame from a prayer candle of The Virgin Mary flickered on the sill.

"Grandma," he sobbed, clutching the hand of the old woman in the bed, her face distorted and puffy from months of chemotherapy. "Grandma, I'm here."

She turned over to him, her pink hat, meant to hide her bald head, askew.

"I left you a cake, it's in the kitchen. You can have some of it when you get home."

"I will Grandma," although he knew no cake waited for him. She'd been in the hospital for weeks since her fall.

"I love you, Grandma."

"Love you too," she said, barely above a whisper.

Stan held nothing, as before.

The firefighter looked up, right into the face of the figure, no anger this time. Resignation. Acceptance.

"You've always been there. It's always been you hasn't it?"

In ways that he could not understand, the figure simply held the thought, and Stan understood;

Yes

"You won't let me save her, will you?"

No

"You're the Angel of Death… Aren't you?"

Yes

Although he took it to mean something more than a fabled reference. A force of nature. An elemental aspect of the universe.

The firefighter willed his body to relax. Despite everything he could humanly do, despite all his training, he couldn't change reality. He let go.

"Will she be happy? Will we… all be happy?"

Yes

He stood up, beholding the scene.

The old woman, now moving despite the scene still being frozen, reached for one of the left pseudopods of the Angel. It formed a hand as if it stuck out of a protective suit. Masculine, with a gold wedding ring.

"I knew you would come for me," she said, serenely. "I've missed you. I love you."

When her hand contacted his, they instantly disappeared. The roar of the fire flooded back into the room, and instinctually Stan donned his facemask.

"STAN! STAN!" cried a voice from behind him.

Spinning around, he assessed the situation. The woman lay in the bed, motionless. Flaming beams had fallen from the ceiling and crushed her frail body, but he knew she had gone long before.

"LET'S GO!" yelled the voice, and the firefighter felt strong arms grab him and pull him out into the living room of the third-floor apartment.

The room cleared now, still fully involved, but with a ventilated ceiling.

In quick succession, Stan was dragged out onto the ladder extending from his rig, brought down, and evaluated by the medics. They quickly strapped an oxygen mask to his face.

"It will be okay, you sit there and relax. Mild smoke. You're lucky." The brown eyes of the EMT peered over her mask at him. He nodded in appreciation.

Moments later the chief sat next to him in the back of the ambulance, settling himself on the wide bumper.

"Hey," he said softly, "the old lady. I'm sorry, we couldn't save her. It's not your fault."

Stan nodded reassuringly at him and took a deep breath of oxygen. She had been saved. He knew it.

The Maw

"You know, you shouldn't stare down it so much. I hear you can go mad from the darkness." Jarred said to me as I stared down into the inky blackness. It felt strange to me like the chasm was trying to pull me in. Or I could fall, tumbling over and over until I ran out of water or starved to death. Jarred was a jerk though.

"What do you know? Who told you that?" I barked back at him, tearing my eyes away from the dark, pink-rimmed hole in the ground.

"Dad said so. He listens to that guy on the wireless."

"The wireless?" I retorted, "Where all of those idiots scream at each other about who is right? Figures, all your dad does is scream anyway."

I instantly regretted it as Jarred hauled off and punched me dead in the shoulder. I didn't cry out. I didn't want to give him the satisfaction, and I guess I deserved it. My arm went numb to the fingers.

"People go there when they die. They get drawn into The Maw by the spirits. They never come back."

"That's stupid," I growled. Everyone knew there were no such things as spirits.

Jarred grabbed my shoulders and feigned pushing me into The Maw. This was impossible, since the wall surrounding it was four feet high and made from quartz, like everything else. I could jump in if I wanted, but you can't push someone in.

"See ya later. Have fun talking to your spirits!" Jarred mocked as he turned and ran between the pink bacteria stalks and toward the open country.

You couldn't eat the stalks without getting really sick, but we could farm vegetables close by. The ground broke up into dirt here, as the roots from the stalks cracked the stone. When the rain fell from the sky we would collect as much as we could to drink and water the crops.

I turned back to the gigantic yawning portal. Most days, mist filled the air above it, and you couldn't see the other side. Other days it was clear and you could see, well nothing. Then there were days where steam filled the opening, billowing out in breaths. Today was a clear day. Motionless and dark. As if it were a painted circle, a kilometer in diameter on the ground, ringed with pink.

I peered down over the edge and felt the warm, humid air drifting up to me.

"Spirits. Bah," I dismissively choked out. "He's a fool."

I stared deep into the expanse and imagined something crawling out; a horrible monster with dozens of legs and a gigantic eye. Terrifying and alien, it reached out over the wall and tore at my cloak, gripping me and tossing me into the void.

I shuddered and shook my head, pulled my cloak up around my ears, and headed back toward the village. I don't normally like to run — I get tired and my vision gets grey — but today I ran through the crops back to our house. The suns shone down overhead, red and blue, but they didn't feel warm at all. They hung there, staring at us in the white sky until they eventually set; this happens on the last day of the year. Those nights are so cold no one goes outside. They feel like they last forever and the only heat comes from The Maw.

As I ran through the vegetables, the soil got rockier until it finally gave way to stone. It stretched from here to the horizon, flat and smooth. Dad told us there was nothing else out there, more of the same, forever.

The village was a collection of houses clustered around the south side of The Maw. Thirty of them, and one hundred and thirteen people. Everyone I knew in the whole world lived right here.

I ran to our cottage past the pots where Dad grew more vegetables and pushed open the metal door. It was warm and dim inside — Dad liked to keep the lights down low to save power — and the quartz walls kept the temperature the same... most of the time. My cheeks buzzed from the rush of blood to the skin. I threw my cloak onto the metal hook by the door.

"Hey Sparkle!" he called from the sink where he washed off vegetables, careful to collect all the dirt so we could put it back onto the fields.

I smiled at his nickname for me.

"Hi Dad," I scanned around. "Where is Mom?"

Dad turned from the sink and smiled at me, his wide grin and stubble revealing several missing teeth, "She's…you know, probably out with her friends or in the fields."

"She's not in the fields Dad."

He sat down at the kitchen table and looked up at me, "I thought I said not to play by The Maw?"

I instantly felt guilty and embarrassed he could figure me out so easily.

"I wasn't playing Dad, I was… studying."

Dad's smile faded with a sigh, he looked like he was trying to think of the right words to say, but he shook his head and smiled weakly.

"What did you see this time?"

"Nothing. As usual."

Dad nodded and got back up from the table. He walked over to the metal cabinets and pulled out metal plates and cups. Instinctively, I helped him set the table, one for each of us, and an empty seat for Grandpa.

"Should we wait for mom?" I asked as Dad took out another bowl of steamed vegetables from the oven.

He tossed the hot bowl onto the table, once again forgetting his silver gloves. He turned and sat down with a groan.

"It's okay, I'm sure she will want us to eat. It's not like she is far," he chuckled softly.

The vegetables smelled great, seasoned with the herbs he grew in the window pots. I tucked into them and ate voraciously.

"Was Jarred there?" he asked between mouthfuls, smirking as he chewed.

It was suddenly too warm in our little quartz cottage, and I tugged at the collar of my sweater.

"I thought so," he took another bite and smirked.

"Dad," I tried to change the subject quickly, "why is it called, The Maw, anyway?"

His eyes rolled up and down, "Sweetie, I thought we went over this…"

We had, I couldn't think fast enough.

"A maw is the open mouth of an animal. Usually a carnivore."

I crunched a bit of broccoli, "Not like us."

"Right, we don't eat meat."

"Nothing eats meat, Dad."

He stopped chewing and blinked away quickly then back at me, his smile ever-widening.

"Yes, my dear, there are no carnivores here."

He had the same expression on his face like when I figured out there was no Sandman.

"So where are there carnivores?"

He drew in a breath as the door opened and Mom sauntered in, she smelled of dirt and plants.

"Darling!" Dad exclaimed, standing to kiss Mom on the cheek. Her eyes closed softly as she threw her strong arms around him.

"Sorry I'm late!" she said, tossing her coat onto the hook, on top of my cloak. "It smells great!" she added drawing up her chair.

"Out with the girls?" Dad asked. After he ate the last spoonful of vegetables in his bowl, a black bean missed his mouth and landed safely in his beard. Mom cleaned her hands in the sink, being careful to collect the soil.

"Those potatoes at Jeanie's place are growing so well! The best way to check is by hand after all." Mom explained as she showed us her sparkling hands, "Jeanie and I added the compost into the soil with the new regolith we processed. I think the combination will work well for tubers."

"How was your day?" Mom turned to ask me.

"Fine, I guess. Jarred and I were…" I completely forgot.

"Playing by The Maw again?" she admonished.

"Mom, I'm not stupid, I'm not going to fling myself into the hole or anything!" I was suddenly angry. I'd told her a thousand times before.

She drew a breath slowly and regarded me with frustrated eyes. Dad leaned back into his chair and watched.

"Sweetie, I'm worried about you. The wall is… small."

"I know Mom. I'm careful."

She shook her head and moved on, adding with a smile, "How is Jarred? Are you two getting on?"

She jumped right in for the kill. Why couldn't she be subtler like Dad?

"He's fine Mom. But… his Dad keeps talking about the wireless. Stupid stories about spirits going into The Maw when we die. Is that true? Are there spirits… down there?" I knew the answer, I was curious to see what she would tell me.

"No one knows what happens when we die. But I'm sure…" She paused and drew a breath, her eyes teared, "I'm sure if spirits existed, and they wanted to go there, they could."

"Is that where Grandpa went?" I motioned to the empty chair.

They both froze in their seats. I've never asked such a question before, but I couldn't hold it back. "Why do we set a place for him? Are we expecting him back?"

"Enough." Dad rose from his seat, the smile gone from his face.

"I'm sorry Mom," I wasn't though. She always avoided his death, saying he died before I was born and nothing more, but I knew it was polite to apologize, and Dad would be all over me if I didn't.

She feigned a smile. I knew I'd upset her. She hurried through dinner and took her plate over to the sink to sort the scraps for compost.

"Well," she started in, "I have to get back over to talk to Jeanie, we have a lecture tomorrow to present our findings."

Dad cleaned up his plate as well, he bumped hips with her, trying to cheer her up. In a few moments, she giggled and leaned over to kiss him, full on the lips. Yuck.

She kissed me on the head and left, and when I turned around Dad stared right at me.

"That wasn't nice, Sparkle."

"Sorry Dad, we all talk about not hiding secrets from each other, but she won't tell me what happened to Grandpa. I'm not a baby."

"She has her reasons. I'm not going to tell you and have her eternally pissed off at me." He chuckled adding a wry smile. "She'll tell you when she's ready."

I hated the fact they were conspiring against me. How much were they lying every day? How was I supposed to understand the truth when I know they lie?

"Okay." I wanted to end the conversation before I got more upset. "Can I go back out?"

"Fine. Don't get into trouble."

I smiled at him. Big and cheesy. Then skipped out the door, grabbing my cloak before it closed.

It was misty when I got out of the cottage; grey and cold. More grey than usual. I headed back to The Maw, to see if it changed.

When I got there, I could barely see the hole, the thick mist and the warm air from inside swirled the clouds around. The sounds of my footfalls bounced back and forth around the bacteria stalks and off the wisps of mist. It made it hard to tell where the noise came from.

I clapped in front of me, over the wall into The Maw. Sharp and quick, the clap came back to me with a whistle. I liked those. I clapped to my left, the sound bounced back off the bacteria stalks sounding like smacking a melon, a dull and water-filled thud. Then at my feet, but the clap came back almost the same as it went. I turned to the right, and before my hands came together, thud. I looked around, thinking Jarred had come over mimicked me again, but I was alone. I raised my hands over my head and brought them together slowly, thud with a rumble.

"What the...?" I glanced at my feet and then the stalks, had one of them fallen?

I raised my hands again, and swung them out into a vee, ready to smash them together with all of my force. As I started pulling them together... BAM!

The noise was deafening, and I was knocked down onto my butt. I glanced up and saw the mist billowing through the bacteria stalks, jetting away faster than I had ever seen anything move. I felt the ground rumbling beneath me; constant, deep, and resonant.

I pulled myself to my feet and stared at the giant hole; mist shot out of it as if being blown with great force, not the breathing I was used to.

Leaning forward, I put my hands on the wall and stood up. The ground around me shook with a rhythmic, boom, boom, boom. It grew stronger and louder.

My mind screamed. I wrenched my body away from the wall and started running, my legs feeling squishy and soft like an over-boiled carrot.

The bangs and rumbles were deafening, and bacteria stalks fell with each thud. I scrambled into the vegetables as quickly as I could. At the edge of the crops, I saw Dad and Jarred screaming at me to run as fast as I could.

Of course, this is when I fell. The soil flew all around me as I tumbled; soil, rock, sky, soil. When I finally stopped, my head landed against a pumpkin, and I turned toward The Maw.

There, the monster from my vision clawed its way out; gigantic legs scrambling for purchase against the soil-covered ground. The wall shattered beneath its great bulk. A singular shining eye sat in the middle of the monster. Dead and lifeless, it glowed with light, pure and white. I couldn't hear anything aside from rumbling and the pounding of blood in my ears. The spirits had come. Or was this the carnivore? Either way, I was dead. My spirit was going to be pulled into The Maw, to join my…

"Dad?" I heard a voice in the distance, quiet and muffled, like a whisper in a dream. Everything moved slowly and turned grey, like when I ran too fast.

"DAD!" the voice called again, louder this time, or was I imagining it? Do voices scream when you die?

"DAD! SPARKLE!" that was my name. The spirits were calling me to my death. I was ready.

"SPARKLE GET UP! It's your grandfather!"

I craned my head up toward my parents. My mom was pointing behind me, crying hysterically as she clutched my dad with her other arm.

I turned back and saw the monster standing right over me; six gigantic legs sitting on their tiptoes, ready to pounce. The light from the eye scattered in all directions, its cold menacing visage impassively staring as if we didn't exist. Its whole body shuddered rhythmically as its steel carapace glinted in the purple sunlight. The next moment I was being lifted to my feet by my dad's strong arms. Mom threw her arms around me so tightly I couldn't breathe.

"Sorry little lady," a voice spoke from the monster; kind, warm, and masculine, yet it sounded like my mother. "I hope you're alright!" it chuckled.

Mom laughed and cried at the same time; Dad smiled. Jarred stood there, looking stupid, but in a cute way.

The white eye instantly grew dark, mist poured from its edges. It opened slowly, like a door left open in the wind, and revealed a man; slender, white beard and hair, his eyes were unmistakably Mom's.

"Grandpa?" I squeaked out as my mother ran past me.

"DAD!" she screamed as she threw herself into the eye and embraced him. His thin arms wrapped around her so tightly they blanched white. I could hear my mother sobbing, loudly, unconcerned with how she sounded.

"It's okay baby," he cooed to her in soft tones. "It's okay. I told you I'd be back."

My grandfather smiled over toward my dad and nodded in recognition, then turned to me and through a tear-soaked face, winked and smiled.

We all walked back to the little cottage, my mother jabbering on like she had never spoken before. I never saw her so happy. Grandpa pointed to all the buildings, asking questions, and making comments. He grabbed the soil, and lifted it to his nose, taking a deep breath. On several occasions he grabbed me around the waist and hugged tight, looking down and smiling broadly. He smelled of plastic, oil, and bacteria stalk, with the slightest hint of my mother.

When we got into the house, he sat down at the head of the table while my mother frantically prepared vegetables on the stove. He pulled up the chair next to him — his chair — and patted it for me to sit down. His warm smile undeniable.

"So, what is your name my dear?" He asked, his sparkling brown eyes staring into mine.

"C — Caroline," I squeaked. "But people call me 'Sparkle.'"

He smiled again, and I realized where the nickname came from. We had the same eyes.

"Pleased to meet you Sparkle, I'm David, your grandfather."

"We thought you were dead Grandpa. We kept this seat open for you in case you came back from…" I realized I was talking way too fast, "… from the dead."

He roared with laughter, and everyone in the cottage laughed as well. I could hear people outside, excitedly talking.

"Please, Grandpa, you have to explain this to me. What happened? Please don't lie."

He sat erect and raised his bushy eyebrows approvingly,

"Smart one here," he commented to my parents, who chuckled to themselves.

"Sweetie," he said to me, his soft eyes swimming. "It must have been hard the last twelve years. Your parents did what they could, and I'm sure they were trying to protect you. In case I never came back. You see…" he paused for effect, "we found this world. We're not from here. We come from a planet with only one sun, a yellow one."

I couldn't believe my ears.

"No lies!" I yelled, desperate to hold back my tears.

"Shh, it's okay baby," he tried to calm me down, exactly like he did with Mom. "This is the truth, our truth. Someone built this planet and then didn't finish the surface. We found it and decided to continue their work. We don't know where they went, or if they will come back.

"When we were ready to settle here, our ship crashed into the exhaust vent, and we went tumbling in. I managed to eject the sleeping pods the people were in, food, and the starter seeds so they could eat. I told them I'd be back."

He gestured around the cottage, "The doors, cabinets, all the metal you see is from those pods. Your parents repurposed them into whatever they needed. They are smart people, like you."

I sat back, agape, I never realized how much the metal was out of place, and I never saw any being made. "The Maw?"

"Maw?" He asked, an expression of genuine concern on his face.

Mom sat down opposite him and slid a plate of vegetables over.

"The Maw is what we call the exhaust vent. It's from the story of…"

"'The Bunnies and The Flower!' How creative!" he laughed again, interrupting her.

"Wait, didn't I hear that story on the wireless?" I asked.

"There are a lot of stories on the wireless, sweetheart," Dad added reassuringly, "…and a lot are not. Nearly all of them have meaning."

Grandpa turned back to me and continued,

"When we finally stopped falling, the navigation system, communications, and the jump ships were ruined. It took us seven years to scavenge the parts enough to repair the crawlers and stay alive. Then another three for me to find a way out. There are so many tunnels!"

"How did you eat? Drink?"

"The planet beneath the quartz is filled with organics. The bacteria stalks live off what breaks away and floats to the surface. It's easy to process those proteins into food."

Mom interrupted, "Ramirez? Brown? Chan? Are they alright?"

Grandpa smiled, "I left them at the ship, the second crawler is with them. We've been in communication the whole time. Now we know the way back to the surface, they will be along soon."

I sat back and took a breath. I had to accept either they were all crazy and I was the only sane one, or they were telling the truth. It fit so easily.

"Why didn't you tell me this?"

Mom glanced at Dad, and then at Grandpa.

"We were going to tell you the truth. When you were old enough." Dad explained, a smile of relief on his face.

I was offended. Deeply. So unfair. I was old enough to figure things out on my own. I was a big girl — a young woman even — I didn't need protection anymore.

I looked around the room again at the teary eyes of my mom, and the warm, calm version on my grandfather. They were different. More real. Like real people instead of just my family.

"Then, The Maw doesn't take spirits away. It's not death. You came back!" I said, finally understanding.

"'Maw' means something else, Sparkle," Grandpa said to me with a reassuring grab of my hand. "What do the baby bunnies in the story call their mother?"

It hit me like getting punched in the face, stronger than anything Jarred would throw.

"That's a baby's story, I don't remem — wait, they call her Maw!"

Grandpa smiled and laughed again, "In one of the languages from where we are originally from sweetie, it's one of the first words anyone says; it means 'mother.'"

Green Sky

Her eyes opened, slowly and painfully. The green-white light of the overhead lamps burned as if she were staring out at the surface of the sun. She blinked and turned away, preparing her body for the pain of consciousness. Steeling herself, she swung out of bed and rested her feet on the cold titanium deck plate. The wall clock read 05:52. Two hours of sleep. More than last night, and definitely more than the first.

Under the clock, a display pulsed a message that she was needed in the medical bay. Again.

The sounds of coughing and creaking bunks told her the others were waking up as well. She had the luxury of having an individual bunk in the Lander — the "Commander's Quarters." Nothing more than a bunk and a closet; a sliding plastic partition denoted its special status. She stood up, slipped on her jumper and socks, and opened the door.

Immediately she could see out of the window opposite her quarters. It sat above the stairwell leading to the lower decks of the Lander and provided natural light into the cone-shaped pod. She and fifty other people called this place home. The light poured in, unchanged since they arrived three days before; cold, dim, and a sickly shade of green that reminded her of bread mold.

The air smelled foul; the mingled scents of body odor, sweaty feet, iron, and methane. The air processors tried to compensate, but the smell always stayed in the air, and condensation from evaporated sweat clung to the walls.

"Good morning, Commander," a hoarse female voice called from the bottom of the central spiral stair.

The Commander looked down and blinked quickly, attempting to focus her dry eyes. Loorea Mitchell, chief planetary geologist, gazed up at her. Her dark brown skin in sharp contrast with her grey jumper.

"The air is bothering you as well, huh?" The Commander asked, barely able to suppress the rasping of her vocal cords.

Loorea answered back, "Yes," she frowned, and then brightened back up, "but at least it is temporary."

The Commander smiled and Loorea made her way through the bustle over to the galley. The main deck served as a staging area, meeting room, and galley. Right now, it was doing all three.

We have to get those habitats built. We won't be able to be cooped up in here for long. She thought.

She skipped the last few stairs, hitting the deck plates hard, her ankles clicking with the strain. Not showing the pain, she pivoted and headed toward the main hatch, passing the food dispensers. One had its main door open, and all manner of tubes snaked in and out of it, broken already. From behind the dispenser a male voice called out.

"Ma'am, don't tell me you aren't going to eat?"

The Commander stopped and turned toward the voice.

"Uh, I guess not?"

He threw a packet to the Commander. She quickly snatched it, surprised at her ability.

"At least try to eat this one, okay?" He called after her and then turned his attention back to the malfunctioning dispenser.

The packet held a dry ration bar, made mostly of soy protein and fat. It also contained a tube of water, ample enough to wash the food down, but not enough to satisfy a thirst. She knew these packets would quickly become rare, and eventually, they would have to start living off the soy grown in the Agricultural Dome. Whenever that was finished.

She climbed down another stair and threw the hatch to the airlock. Here the methane and iron smell overwhelmed her, and she wasn't sure if her stomach turned because of the smell, or the absolute hunger.

She stopped and looked around. The Med Bay hatch was closed, the airlock empty, and no one descended the stair. She ripped open the packet, ate the protein bar, and hurriedly washed it down with the water. Checking around again, she stuffed the empty packet in a pocket and wiped her face. One less. It barely took the edge off the hunger. She had to stretch the rations as much as possible, and if that meant eating every other day, then so be it.

Reaching out, she pressed the door contact and opened the Med Bay hatch. As it opened, she witnessed a med-tech pulling a sheet over the body that lay on the bay's examination table.

She froze. The reality of the death hit square to the soul. As if the last nine billion weren't enough. Every death meant one less person to help keep humanity alive.

"Was it…?" she croaked out to the tech.

The sturdy Chinese face of the med-tech turned away from the body and up at the Commander.

"Old age, stress, new planet. Take your pick. But yes, the compound fracture in his leg probably didn't help."

The Commander stared absently at the wound; blood-covered bits of flash-frozen flesh, a jagged snapped femur, torn seams.

"Did he have any family, ma'am?" the tech asked.

"No," replied the commander, shaking out of her reverie. "At least not anymore."

"I see," the tech turned off his monitor and stepped away from the body. He asked in a quieter tone, "you know, we never established a procedure for what to do with the deceased."

She never thought about it. She was so focused on keeping all the colonists alive, there was never a consideration of what to do if someone were to pass on. Quickly, she became pragmatic.

"Is the suit functional?" she asked the tech.

"It can be repaired."

The Commander took a breath, "strip the suit, wrap him in his sheet and store the body in the empty rover container next to Cargo 1."

She realized that must have sounded incredibly harsh, although the tech made no sign of it. "Until we can have a ceremony for him in the Ag Dome. When it's finished."

"Yes ma'am," the tech uncovered the body and started removing his pressure suit.

"Well, I'm glad we have a procedure now," stabbed the icy voice of Specialist Morrison from the other side of the Med Bay.

The Commander snapped her head around, unaccustomed to being addressed so.

"Ma'am," Morrison added, with much delay.

"Is there a problem, Specialist?" the ranking officer asked, stripping all the emotion from her voice.

"Yes Commander, there is."

The Commander took a long step toward the Specialist. She stood with her, staring down at her fierce gaze. "And?"

"Well, ma'am, Since Chief Brown is gone, we are now left without our best hydrologist. How are we going to find water without him?"

"I guess you will have to make do."

The Specialist bristled.

"See if you can find someone with similar interests and get them to assist you. I hereby give you the field rank of Chief Hydrologist."

Morrison stood speechless, after a long moment she bowed perfunctorily and walked quickly out of the Med Bay.

"I don't envy your job," said the tech, removing the final bit of suit from the body.

The Commander turned back and then looked down at the naked, blood-covered corpse.

"Nor I yours."

Black Mask

As part of my daily break from the grind in the post-pandemic world, I took my usual walk around The Battery. Of course, nothing is the same as it used to be. The crush of humanity, even for lower Manhattan, had grown distant though the quarantines had been lifted. Blue masks adorned many of the passers-by. Groups gathered in small clusters, family groups, couples, close friends. When disparate groups intersected, it became obvious they were giving each other space. Then the extreme case of joggers running, blue masked, blue gloved, some wearing eye protection. Parents with babies in strollers, hermetically sealed against the world. A generation of babies in bubbles. I shrugged; this is New York after all. It takes all types.

I leaned against the rail, looking east past the Statue of Liberty and out of the Narrows to the ocean. I could feel the cool October breeze kicking over the water. Welcoming and relaxing, with a hint of chill. We were lucky this year, nature spared us another massive storm.

Out of the corner of my left eye, I noticed someone else leaning against the railing. They weren't there when I arrived, they must have shown up while I engaged in my reverie. Female. Average height, average build. Black hair. Wearing a black N-95 mask, with plastic vents on either side. As with so many men, the side-eye glance gave me enough information to make it worth an approach. Being nonchalant I turned toward the Narrows again, then shifted my body toward hers, finally turning my head in her direction. She had gone.

"Crap," I lamented under my breath. I searched around quickly to see if I could catch a glimpse of her moving off. Hopefully, she will settle again some other place, or she had been with someone and I didn't notice and went off with them. I kept searching and not finding her. After a few seconds, I let go of the notion and went back to surveying the harbor. There would be others. I tried to reassure myself.

My watch beeped to remind me I had to get back to work and earn my keep. Most of us worked from home these days, and we enjoyed getting out when needed, but there were still bills to pay, and scenery didn't write the checks.

Half a day later with work finished, I walked out of my apartment so I could catch the last rays of sunshine before the long autumn night stretched in. I walked up to Chelsea to hit the market and my favorite pizza place. Not the best pizza in this city famous for it, but I liked the vibe, and after months of quarantine, I needed the hike. I stepped in and surveyed the room; crowded, but not oppressively so. Again, social distance, small clusters of people, no mingling. I ordered a slice from the stall to my left, nodded hello to the attendant who I'd come to know over the years. Asked him how the family had been doing, etc. The kind of small talk you make when you like the person, but don't want to dig.

At 7:00 the announcement came in over the P.A. for the daily moment of silence, asking us to remember all the lives lost and the efforts of essential workers who put their lives on the line day in and day out. I whipped off my hat and cast my eyes to the floor, which I couldn't see anyway behind my blue mask. There wasn't any announcement, only a soft electronic bell, then another softer one at 7:01. You could hear some of us silently sob, others making no noise respectfully, and still others busy plucking away on their cellphones. It changed from the cheering we'd done in the early days. It felt more somber, as if we were collectively dealing with the shock, finally. We ignored the children who didn't understand, and I silently prayed they never had to go through this again.

When I looked back up, I saw her walk past me out of the door. The place where I stood practically blocked the doorway to Chelsea Market. How did anyone get past me without me noticing?

"Black mask," I said behind mine and darted out of the door to catch her. I looked up and down 16th, but I didn't see her again. I went seriously far from The Battery, on purpose, and I still ran into her. I tried to figure the odds but left it as "weird."

I grabbed my pizza from the counter and quickly glanced at my friend. His mask had the logo for Chelsea Market on it. A cow in profile, white, emblazoned across a burgundy mask.

I went to bed that night trying to figure out the situation. I had a few hypotheses which fit the facts; seeing the same person, being followed, an ex stalking me. Or am I overthinking a coincidence? After a short while, I gave up and promptly fell asleep.

The next morning, a Saturday, I executed a test: get as far away from my apartment by as many routes as possible. I grabbed the 1 at Rector Street, rode it to Times Square, and switched to the Q — looking around constantly and switching cars every time we stopped. I took the Q to 96th, got off, and walked through Central Park. I went down Central Park West, over to 66th, and to Lincoln Center. I walked past the fountain to the back of the plaza, leaned against the Met, and watched. I scanned the crowd for hours. People must have thought me insane.

After a while, my feet ached, and I started getting hungry. Extremely hungry. I walked to the street vendor to get a pretzel, looking around like a paranoid madman. There was always a palpable paranoia in the city, we were all still jumpy. But I acted weird. A police officer, blue masked, walked up to me, keeping social distance.

"You alright, Sir?" he asked, forceful but also concerned.

I choked and stammered, "Sorry officer, I waited too long to eat, blood sugar."

He nodded quickly, "You gonna be okay? You need to sit?" He asked, relaxing, but also spreading his stance to catch me if I fell.

"I'm fine, honestly." I popped my mask down under my chin and took a big bite of the stale pretzel, making sure I made a show of getting mustard on my cheeks. I smiled and showed him the pretzel. He nodded and turned back toward the plaza.

"Geez, August," I said to myself. "Get a grip."

I finished the pretzel, downed the water I also purchased and threw the bottle into the recycling. It bounced out, of course, and I bent down to get it. The corner of my eye caught a glimpse across the street at Dante Park. There she stood.

I tore into the street, not taking my eyes off her. She stared right at me, her pale blue eyes locked onto mine. I couldn't feel my feet, my vision tunneled straight at her. My breathing drowned out all else. I guess that's why I didn't hear the bike messenger screaming at me.

When I came to, I could see the buildings arching into the sky above me, as I lay flat down on my back in the middle of Columbus Avenue. The police officer held up my head, yelling.

"Hey! Talking to you! What's your name?"

I groaned out, "August… Bu… August Buchanan."

"Mister Buchanan, what the hell were you doing?!?"

"I saw someone, a friend. I… I wasn't paying attention."

"You weren't paying attention? You walked out into the street! Whadda you, a kid?" His voice no longer conciliatory, anger seethed, I deserved it.

"Do you need an ambulance?" He asked, partially barking.

"No, sir," I said, honestly realizing how stupid I had been acting, "I'm sorry, I crashed too hard with the sugar rush."

I sat up and looked around, the police officer's blue gloved hands going under my arms to hold me steady. The messenger had gone, along with my 'friend'.

"You got a place to go? You need to go home," he said. Not asking, more like a command.

"Battery Park City."

He helped me to my feet and flagged a cab.

"Go home and get some rest," he said. Enunciating every word clearly and loudly. "Battery Park City," he ordered to the cabbie.

"Yes, sir," I squeaked as I ducked into the back of the cab. "I'm sorry."

"Yeah," he said dismissively as he closed the door.

I closed my eyes as the cab took me back to The Battery. Maybe it had been the stress of the last couple of years; it had come out and I started hallucinating. I've heard when you're under stress it usually shows up when you finally relax. Could this be the new "relaxed?"

When we got close to home, I pointed to the park. The cab pulled over and I got out, tapping my phone to the meter to pay. I took a deep breath, checked my mask, and walked back to the railing.

People were still in tight groups. No mingling. It felt colder than it used to, less personable and keeping their distance, more than the six feet they were supposed to. I looked at the Statue again, staring at the point where I knew her feet were standing on broken chains. The setting sun casting a blue shadow through the clouds. Blue. Surgical mask blue.

"Why are you following me?" I didn't even glance up. I knew she would be there.

"Because you are important Mr. Buchanan."

I took another breath, keeping my lips pursed so I didn't suck in my mask.

"Why?" I asked slowly, turning my face toward hers.

Her cold blue eyes stared back at me over the black mask.

"Because, you can stop all of this," she said coldly.

"All of what?"

I looked around at the tight knots of people. We were recovering. We were jittery, still getting used to the new normal, nothing more. At least that is what I wanted to tell myself and believe. The world changed so much, and I knew it would never go back to how it used to be.

"This is not over. The virus will never be this strong again, but it stays with us forever. Life will never be the same. We become more separated, more distant, more paranoid. Our culture stops growing, we become afraid. You've already seen it, it's not only the virus, its... everything."

"Why are you telling me this in the past tense?" I said, bracing for the insane answer I knew had to be coming. I heard the individual words come out from behind the mask, slowly and painfully.

"Because, I am from the future," she said. Coldly. Calculatingly. Matter of fact.

I leaned back against the railing and drew my gaze up and down over her frame. "I wouldn't be able to tell you were crazy by looking at you. Usually, stalkers don't wait long before they pounce, if they pounce at all. What gives?"

"I had to make sure I knew it was definitely you before I approached. I had to be sure."

"I don't see a Terminator about to strike. Why don't you tell me another one?" I'd had it. I turned on my heel to head back to my apartment.

"You can stop this," again, coldly, at my back. "It gets worse. This is the beginning. Everything changes from here. We do not take the right path."

I spun around, enraged, quivering. I didn't want to go exploring my repressed emotions with some madwoman on the street.

"How?!" I yelled. "How do I stop this, you psycho? What's the right path?"

She walked up to me, close enough I could feel the heat from her body.

I jumped back reflexively; I had not been this close to someone in over a year. Not since…

"You see?" She said quietly. "You can't shake it. It does not go away. You never get close to someone again."

"And how do I fix it?"

"You are the only person," she whispered, eyes darting, "who never gets infected."

"What? We still aren't all tested yet."

"We contact traced you. You came into contact directly with no fewer than seventeen symptomatic cases. All of them died. Yet you never got sick. You also did not acquire antibodies. The old records are specific, you are pristine."

I stood back, mind reeling. She had to be nuts. "And?" Trying again to hold back my emotions.

"And we can see what is unique about you. Your DNA."

She reached up and grabbed my elbow, her eyes boring into me. Fear and revulsion tore through my body, as I tried to pull back. But I also loved the feeling. A hand on my arm. Not alone. Warmth.

"We know who patient zero is. We can inoculate them. More than a vaccine, we can stop this before it starts."

"What about Smallpox? Polio? Spanish Flu? They killed so many more."

Why did I go along with this insanity?

"We didn't know how it started then, or anyone with innate immunity. The data on you are sound."

I worked my way out of her hand, but my heart didn't slow.

"Whatever. I'm going."

"I can't force you… unfortunately. But we need you. We cannot go down this path. We don't learn."

I stared at her. Incredulous and immobile. Behind her, a mother shrieked when a little girl hugged another from a strange family. She saw a new friend; her mother saw a threat.

"You're here, aren't you? We survived and so much more happened. Should we erase that? Besides, you being here changes the future, doesn't it? We can learn. Adapt. Change for the better. My present is not your future!"

"I cannot stay. You need to make a decision before it is too late, and we will not be able to take you with us." She reached for my head as if to pull my hat off or grab some hair, and I jerked away, smacking the back of my skull into a tree. I quickly shook it off and turned back. She had disappeared, completely gone. Back and forth I searched, nothing. There is no way she could have disappeared that fast, she had been just here.

I glanced back toward the Statue, then at the empty park. I took another look around for her. The sun had set, and a cold breeze blew off the water, all the while my clothes were soaked to the skin from sweating.

I tried to move, willing my feet to slide forward. I looked down to assess their lack of progress.

There, on the flagstone at my feet, a black, N-95 mask.

Even Aliens Like Quiet Sometimes

A cool breeze blew through the trees and rustled their purple leaves softly. The backyard was peaceful. Thoram Kelmar lifted his head toward the great globe of the gas giant called Alpha. The data stream flowed into his eyepiece, showing all the forms of electromagnetism pouring from the body. In a synthetic brilliance his eyes could not normally comprehend, he could see all the minute detail of the great world. At least as interpreted by the data relays buried in the ground all across the planet. Soft words whispered in his ears. Information and data of every imaginable kind. It all came pouring in.

He closed his eyes and braced himself against the inevitable shock about to overcome him. He took off his eyepiece and pulled out his earbuds. The world fell silent and black.

Darkness enveloped him, but he could feel his eyes straining to make out shapes. Slowly his ears noticed the hum of insects and the rustling of leaves. He sat there staring up to where he knew Alpha would be, and slowly, ever so slowly, a faint green circle resolved into view. Around the dim shape, stars shone brilliantly against the backdrop of night.

He kept telling his nervous system to relax and embrace the change. He felt calmness slowly overtake him. The full sounds of his backyard on a warm summer night filled his ears; the smell of the dirt, the feel of the breeze on his skin, and the faint green hue of Alpha overhead. Finally, at peace. He so rarely felt it these days.

He knew there would be a few minutes before the sun would return from behind Alpha, and the afternoon and all its distractions would resume.

One more stolen moment.

He felt a tapping on his leg and his spine reflexively reacted; it took all of his concentration not to swat the tapping away. He steadied his breath again and grunted slightly.

"Father?" came a quiet voice.

He grunted again.

"Father, is there something the matter?"

"Not at all."

"There must be something wrong why have you disconnected yourself was lunch not adequate did I not prepare it for you properly are you and mother fight..."

With rising frustration, Thoram raised his hand.

"Pause. Personality consideration."

Thoram looked down, there, cuddled around his right leg stood a creature resembling a cross between a rabbit and a monkey. It was small, the size of a large cat, its fur stark white. It gazed up at him with oversized gold-irised eyes. Downturned whiskers glowed softly with alternating blue and white pulses. Its ears, similarly downturned, framed its face in a heart shape.

After Thoram finished his sentence, the creature changed its demeanor. The ears perked up, the whiskers straightened themselves and glowed a solid blue. The eyes, however, did not change color.

It spoke again in a soft child-like voice, indeterminate of sex.

"I am sorry father I forget you require..." It forced itself to pause. "You require 'alone time' although I still do not understand why you would want to separate yourself from the rest of us it seems to be lacking a kind of socialization I cannot fathom..." Its voice rapidly sped up from its forced pause.

Thoram cut it off again, in a patient, and yet increasingly more stern voice.

"Dax."

The sad face returned.

"Everything is fine. I have told you not all sentient beings on this planet need to be connected at the same time. You will not understand the reason, but you must accept the fact." He smiled at Dax, and it instantly perked up again.

"I will remember father." It forced a pause again. Its whiskers were vibrating and pulsing quickly this time and a barely audible purr came from its throat.

"Will you be returning to the house when the eclipse is over?"

"Yes, I will be right there."

Dax sat on its back feet and patted Thoram's leg where it had been clutching him in concern. Its whiskers flashed green briefly and then it trotted back into the house.

Thoram turned back up at Alpha, as a bead of brilliant red light broke over the limb. He closed his eyes and let the warm light shine on his face. A moment later his data inputs beeped and flashed wildly — he was needed.

Cold Hudson

Sunlight shines down through the azure sky. The water, normally grey-green, takes on a bluish hue. Like little sapphires being scattered with every wave. The breeze is not quite blowing white caps, but it's also not calm. Enough to make you queasy if you aren't paying attention, but not enough to lose your balance.

Behind, the dock of Paulis Hook bangs against the quay. Another ferry pulls in, slamming its bow against the pylons. The captain keeps the engine at half speed. It's not worth the time or the effort to tie up the boat. It will be loaded and on its way again in three minutes. Patient customers boarded with competitive ease; it's not crowded. There is no reason to jockey for a "good seat." It's the middle of the day and, despite the cold, it's a festive mood. After a minute, the crew ties up the gangway and the captain pulls the ferry away from the dock, giving the perfunctory safety instructions before turning the boat toward the opposite shore and gunning the engine.

To the left, the grey expanse of the Hudson River stretches up to the George Washington bridge. Jersey City and Hoboken on the left, Manhattan on the right. Helicopters buzz by overhead, like bees going from flower to flower. Occasionally the sunlight catches the rotors, and a brilliant blue-white flash bounces down onto the river. Under them is the nearly constant boat traffic from ferries, tugs, small cargo ships, and coast guard patrol boats. This display is nowhere near the heyday of the harbor before the airplane, but it is enough to make you remember — despite the bridges and tunnels — this is a sea town.

To the right, looking down the river and out to the sea, the Statue of Liberty holds her light and faces outward toward Europe. If you squint hard enough, or if the binoculars on deck are working, you can see her stepping away from the broken shackles at her feet. Her toga raising in the back as she takes a step both full of ease and yet determination. Confident in her mission to enlighten the world. Her ever-present, unblinking visage cast upon the horizon.

Breaking the horizon line, the rigid grey beams and arches of the Verrazzano-Narrows Bridge cuts across like a knife, binding the southern boroughs with what was once the largest span in the world. Ducking under the deck reveals the vanishing point, the infinite dot the ancients assumed meant the Earth stretched on forever. You can forgive them their ignorance; it's breathtaking.

Ahead, the intended destination looms large. The vast expanse of lower Manhattan dominates the sky. The sun, nearly overhead, lights the spires in an ethereal light. Sunlight is bounced from nearly every pane of glass, and the city glows in its radiance. So much is presented it nearly overwhelms the senses. You breathe deeply and take in the entirety of the moment. The rocking, the crisp morning air, the coffee taste still on your lips and mouth, your stomach filled with this morning's bagel.

The sun beats on your face; you close your eyes and turn toward it.

The captain announces the ferry is about to arrive.

Centre Hallow

"Professor?" I heard the voice from behind me, but I didn't listen.

Trying to get through the lab door, I barely registered him. This new building had so many labs, and hallways — one after another. I have worked on this campus for the last fifteen years, but this building had been built recently. For whatever reason, I'd never taught a class here until today.

I was searching for the "Heightmeyer" side of the building and a lab on the fourth floor. I kept pulling at the handle and swiping my card. It wouldn't budge.

"Professor?" Again, behind my head. I could hear the concern in his voice.

I turned around quickly, trying to not let the frustration show.

"What?!" I snapped, completely unsuccessful.

The grad student stepped back, eyes darting.

"I'm sorry," I shook my head quickly, hoping the admission would sink in — without having to explain too much.

"No, it's fine," he said, pushing his glasses up. "What room are you looking for?"

"Heightmeyer 416," I said, with no preamble.

"Ah, yeah, that's on the west side of the building, fourth floor. This is east, four."

I stopped for a second — an eternity under the caring yet penetrating gaze of the student. I *was* in the west side… wasn't I?

Sensing my confusion, he spoke up, "This building is big. The numbering changes after the bridge. Happens all the time. You have to get used to it."

I turned back around to the door, studying it this time. A large yellow placard with red lettering below my eye level read: "Hightower, 327, E4."

No anger here, only the resignation that I, again, went too fast and didn't pay attention to everything right in front of me. I glanced down at my watch: 1:12 pm.

"You need to go down the stairs to the left here, across the bridge, then back up. It's on the right. It doesn't connect on four."

"Thanks," I said curtly.

I turned and sprinted toward the door. Well, at least whatever you can call sprinting in wingtips and a sport coat. Pushing the door open, I willed myself to slow down a bit. The last time I didn't and I broke the hinge. Physics is real, and I ignored it at my peril, often.

I threw the door open and slipped into the cool stairwell without waiting for the door to fully open. The concrete walls echoed the slamming door harshly, the dull buzz of the fluorescent lights my only greeting.

"Down one, the bridge, up one."

I hurried down the stairs quickly; already twelve minutes late for class. Right now, all the students will be throwing about the lore of "Ten minutes for a professor, fifteen for a master's, twenty for a doctor." Which has never been true. But every year like the spring crocus it pops back up. I can remember my undergrad twenty years ago and still remembered all the tricks.

Opening the door to the bridge the emptiness stretched before me. Trying to stay dignified I hurried, useless though with all my sweating and panting, I couldn't hide it from anyone.

I bolted across the bridge. The sun shone brightly through the glass walls, and it hurt my eyes by contrast of the darkened stairwell. Momentarily blinded, I went for the door on the opposite side of the bridge. I threw it open toward me, narrowly missing my face in the process. Catching a glimpse of the clock in the stairway, it read 1:15.

"They get extra credit if they stayed," I commented between quick breaths.

"Up one." I flew up the stairs and reached for the door, contacting the cool metal, stopping dead.

Behind me, I heard the slightest sob. Quietly unobtrusive. Like a kitten, but I instantly recognized it.

Spinning around, I saw a little girl sitting on the stairs up to the next level. A young face stared up at me, five or six years old, with disheveled walnut brown hair. When she realized my presence, she jerked herself to stand. Tears and mucus streaked down her face and her startling olivine eyes bathed in an ocean of swollen red.

My heart pounded in my chest from exertion, surprise, concern for this little girl, and the fact I'd never make it to class.

I quickly bent down, to get my eye level the same as hers, my knees cracking.

"Hey sweetie," I said quietly, with as much control as I could muster. "What are you doing here by yourself?"

She recoiled as if in trouble, hardly what I intended, but the sudden appearance of an authority figure can be unsettling.

"Shhhh, it's alright." My heart ached for this little one. "What is your name honey? Where are your parents?"

"I — I want my mommy." Again through a sob, "My mommy."

I wanted to pluck her up and carry her to the end of the Earth to find her mother, I also didn't want to freak her out. I'm a strange man to her and this is an enclosed space.

"Sweetheart, I can help you. My name is Kevin. I teach here. Let's go find Mommy, okay?" I extended my hand to her, which still shook from all the adrenaline.

Reluctantly she took it and looked up at me with frightened eyes. "Okay," She squeaked. "I can't open the door."

I stood and scanned the metal door, a card access panel on the side of it. Which I didn't notice coming in, of course.

"Ah!" I said and smiled down at her, producing my ID with my other hand.

She smiled at me, nearly beaming.

"What's your name sweetie?" I asked her, as I slid the ID card into the slot.

"Darlene," she replied, becoming more chipper.

"Okay, Darlene. Let's go find Mommy."

I opened the door to a long hallway with classrooms on either side, quiet with class in session. I could hear the minutes ticking away. The first day of class and a lecture, so the TA would be waiting on me as well.

"Is your mommy on this floor, Darlene?"

Darlene held my hand tight but swung back and forth as we walked, much more relaxed, and of purposed mind.

"Mommy isn't here. She's busy. Ms. Jackson takes care of me."

Confused in the way only child can confuse you, I asked, "Ms. Jackson is…?"

"Ms. Jackson is a nice lady. She takes care of all of us. We all got here the same way."

Presuming she meant some kind of childcare I inquired, "Is she in this building?"

Darlene stopped in her tracks and regarded me with the *are you stupid?* expression, common to their kind.

"Right. Silly me."

"All of my friends are there. Sophia, Elijah, Lin-Sun, Skylar, Nithany, Mildred…"

She prattled on so many names I lost count, and occasionally interjected, "Uh-huh."

We continued down the long hallway and turned the corner. I heard a chorus of children behind a frosted glass door which quelled my rising concern.

"WE'RE HERE!" Darlene practically vibrated out of my hand.

She stopped and stared up at me as if analyzing my features.

"Thank you, Mr. Kevin. My mommy will love you. You're a nice man."

She grabbed the door handle and jumped into the room, closing it quickly behind. The children cheered, and then dropped to whispers.

My watch beeped; the TA texting me.

"Professor? Are you coming?"

I tapped back an "OK!" and tore back down the hallway.

In a full run, I grabbed the handle to the door, catching a glance, a placard above the door read: "Third Floor, Heightmeyer."

"What? I'm on the wrong floor?"

I reached for the door handle and pulled it toward me, but I realized too late someone was coming in the other way. I couldn't stop its progress, nor warn the other person. It hit me square in the face. Everything went black.

Why are my teeth throbbing? Blood? What…?

My eyes flickered open and searing white light flooded in. Fluorescent. Formaldehyde. Definitely a bio lab. Anatomy I thought from the vague smell of organs. Empty though.

"What time is it?" I called out, not sure to whom, deliriously talking to the air.

"Easy there, Champ," a woman's calm and relaxed voice spoke to me.

My lip hurt more. Cold and burning at the same time.

"I'm wet? Ice pack." It all came back. I sat up, holding the pack against my lip.

"It's 1:35, I think they went home. Twenty-minute rule and all," she said with a laugh.

I focused on her strawberry blonde hair pulled back up into a ponytail, green eyes. Pastel blue lab coat. I'd never seen her before. "Hi," I croaked out. "Who hit me?"

"A grad student. They said they were sorry but couldn't miss class."

"Not one of mine?" I joked and got to my feet. The room swam a bit, but I could manage.

"No, I thought I could take care of you though, I am a doctor after all."

The inside joke among the biology doctorates. None of us are medical doctors, but we know how the body works.

She got up with me to make sure I didn't topple over. Her petite frame would be completely useless if I did fall, but I liked the thought. Normally I tell anyone assisting me if I fall to let me go. At six and a half feet, if I drop, I'm taking them with me. She was so earnest to help though, her small, warm hands pressed up against my back so determinedly.

"Thank you… Florence?" I quipped.

She smiled wryly. "It's Pamela actually, but I think I might like that."

I raised an eyebrow and grinned. Torn between talking to my beautiful savior, and running to class, I needed to move.

"Well, Pamela, thank you for the patch up," I intoned, trying to find a way to gracefully exit the conversation. Not that I wanted too.

"I've got to get to class, or they will eat me alive. I'm going to let you get back to your day here."

Again, the wry smile, with the slightest hint of disappointment; I've never regretted a decision so quickly in my entire life.

"Right, I'm sure something around here is demanding my attention." She gestured to the empty lab. "Nice meeting you, Champ."

"Likewise, Florence." I smiled at her and bowed slightly.

I turned to the door to leave and realized I still had no idea of my location.

"Heightmeyer, 316, W3," she said without prompting.

"Right," I said, embarrassed.

"Biology," she added without me asking what department I stood in, with a hint of snark flavoring the word.

I smiled at her quick wit and tipped back out of the door.

"Right. W4?"

She pointed to the ceiling. "Upstairs."

"Thanks." I very quickly stole a glance at her left hand. No ring.

"Can I repay you sometime? Coffee? Grilled Sticky?" I asked.

"The Diner closed down remember? No Stickies."

Damn.

"But we can hit The Creamery. I'll buy." She offered.

"When…?"

"Four o'clock. Thursday."

I liked this woman.

I'm not going to lie and say I wasn't thinking of next Thursday all week. But I also needed to focus on things like teaching and general life tasks. The summer session has to be my favorite, so much more relaxed than the regular semester, and I always volunteered to teach. Yet I wondered why I never got my research done.

It took an eternity until Thursday arrived, when it did, I quickly headed down to the Creamery; location of the best ice cream in Pennsylvania. Some would argue the best on the planet, biased, I agreed of course.

While waiting for Pamela to show, I noticed a group of children playing in the grass next to The Creamery, out of the way of the lines of patrons. Kids playing in the grass here is nothing unusual, everyone in Centre County ended up here at one point or another. Unusually though, some of the children seemed to be in costume. Nineteenth-century attire, 1950's, 1980's, and even a few Susquehannock children in traditional clothing. Not cheap costume knockoffs, quite good. Authentic even. Something must have been going on in town and they came back here to celebrate. Maybe the drama club? I didn't pay much attention to what happened in town, college towns were all the same: loud, a lot of students, too much alcohol, not my kind of place. It existed in the periphery of my mind.

Darlene played in the group, and she waved when she noticed me staring. I waved back and the rest of the children giggled and waved; sweet and silly, I laughed despite myself. Some of the other customers looked around to see what engaged me but dismissed it. Shrubbery lined the picnic tables, probably obscuring their view.

I watched the kids regardless; they were playing some game I didn't understand, not meant for me anyway. A woman, about twenty, shepherded the children. She too wore somewhat antiquated clothing; like something my mother would have worn in "her time" in the 1970s. Ms. Jackson, I presumed.

Darlene smiled happily, all the shock of the early part of the week had gone. She pointed over my shoulder excitedly and I turned and saw Pamela walking up to me. Lab coat off, sunglasses. Her strawberry blonde hair, still in the ponytail, bounced in the light breeze. In this relaxed setting, I barely recognized her.

"Hey there," I said, trying to be nonchalant, leaning against the wall. She smiled, walked right up, and hugged me.

Excitement shivered up and down my spine, not expecting her to be so forward with me. I did not protest at all.

"Hey Champ, how's the lip?"

"The best person possible nursed me back to health," I said, tilting my head down at her, seeing my reflection in her wayfarers. "My own personal Florence Nightingale."

She smiled wryly.

"You never told me your name."

She stepped back. Did she smell like vanilla, or could it be the ice cream?

"I didn't? Seriously?" I desperately tried not to let my embarrassment show.

I glanced around feigning caution, "How do I know I can trust you with that kind of information?"

"You were out cold for two minutes, you think I couldn't figure it out, Kevin?"

It took me completely aback. I stood flabbergasted.

"H — How did you know?" I could see in her glasses I appeared about as stupid as I sounded.

She took off the shades and stared at me with the same regard Darlene gave me. Windex blue eyes smiling.

"Your ID was in your hand. I checked obviously."

I really liked this woman.

"Oh, man. You are dangerous. I'm gonna have to keep my guard up with you, lest you take advantage of me."

Again, the wry smile.

"Then I'm going to take advantage of your sweet tooth." She said walking away from me and grabbing the handle of the door, putting her hand on it about face height for me, and winking. She mocked me, sending my heart racing.

"What's your flavor?" She asked.

"Bittersweet Mint. As if there is another flavor?"

"Death by Chocolate, of course."

I smiled and grabbed the door to follow her in.

Glancing back, I checked on Darlene and her friends, but they were gone.

"So how long have you been teaching here?" She asked me later as we walked past the football stadium. Darkened during the summer session, with enough lights to remind you there were one hundred thousand people here a few months ago. It felt as if the building itself mourned the loss of all the cheering and activity.

I thought back and added the years up.

"I did undergrad and grad school here, so…" I pretended to count on my fingers. "I dunno, since the Carter Administration. How long ago is that?"

I hoped she'd get the joke I was a child at the time. She pushed against my arm and I bobbled my ice cream, catching it before it fell to the ground.

I laughed and caught my balance.

"There is no need for violence, my dear!" I said, feigning umbrage.

"I can fix you if you break," she said, stopping and gazing up at me. That look. The look a woman gives you when you know she has made her decision. Only a fool or a coward would sit around and psychoanalyze it, "analysis paralysis." I instinctually leaned in for the kiss.

It wasn't the ice cream — she did smell of vanilla. Soft and warm, with chocolate notes. She breathed deep, and I could feel her chest rise to meet me. My head swam. My heart pounded. My body flooded with both excitement and warmth; relaxed yet on fire. Nothing existed in the universe at this moment. Just me, her, and a stadium designed to hold a hundred thousand spectators.

A soft smile spread across her soft lips, a bit of chocolate in the corner I dared not tell her about lest I kill the moment.

"I think it could do the trick, yeah." I said, trying to keep the adrenaline from betraying my cool exterior.

The wry smile again, and a playful slap across my cheek. Yep. I could not deny her.

"Careful Florence," I said. "I might like it."

Like a vice, her arm tightened around my waist, likewise, I did the same and pulled her in, pressing her body against mine. In my mind, I could hear the stadium cheering for us.

Later in the evening, I walked her back to her car. I don't like to use the word "giddy" but I can't think of anything more appropriate. I could barely feel my feet as I walked and almost skipped beside her, desperate to hold back my enthusiasm. Her hand in mine and my lips sore and raw, but with so many feel-good hormones, I barely registered it.

We leaned on the car in the empty parking deck talking about anything and everything. We were both divorcés and were focused on our research; I didn't ask specifics, we knowingly sidestepped getting into that conversation too early. She'd done her post-doc here after coming from Iowa State a few years back. We simply did not run into each other. This hardly said much considering I didn't socialize with many faculty. Being single at my age always made me feel like a fifth wheel and I preferred other, less pathetic, forms of attention.

My watch buzzed at 10:30. My "you should be in bed" alarm.

"Um, sweetie, I hate to be that guy..." I started in, as she suppressed a yawn.

She looked at me with sleepy eyes. Content and tired, she nodded.

"Where do you live anyway?" I asked hoping she didn't have far to drive.

"Centre Hall."

Relieved, I sighed. The next town over, a few miles away, nothing to worry about. "You gonna be okay?"

"I'm a big girl, thank you," she said playfully as she swung around and into the car seat. "I'll text you when I get in."

She closed the door and rolled down the window. I leaned in and kissed her for the hundredth time.

"I had a great time," I said.

"I still am," she said, adding her grin that melted my knees.

She drove away, swiping her badge through the gate, waving from the window.

The parking gate creaked when it closed behind her. Strangely it sounded weird, like giggling.

I spent so much time talking to her on the phone, I felt like a teenager. I loved that week. Pamela had been doing research this semester and I taught a full load. So, I found myself letting class go early and rushing down to her lab to catch her before her post-docs showed up and demanded her attention.

She invited me over to her place Saturday, offering to make me a German dish I had never eaten before. Something with sausages and potatoes. I gave up meat for health reasons, but I told her I would make the exception this time. Although she didn't have to go the whole "traditional woman" route here when I suggested it she insisted. Who was I kidding, I'd go kill a cow with my bare hands if she asked me to.

Having not seen Darlene for a few days I went to go see how they were doing right after Pamela went in and subdued her students. I'm sure she told Ms. Jackson about me. I tried to remember how many doors it took to get there. I didn't pay attention the first time but I remembered the only one with frosted glass.

Turning down the hallway I saw it again on the right, listened for the children, but heard nothing. The dark frosting hinted at an empty room. Could it be their nap time? Were they watching something? I had no idea what they were doing, but I didn't want to disturb them. I turned on my heel and left.

Back at Pamela's lab — oncology research — the door stood open and I used it to my advantage.

"Professor?" I asked, being as professional as possible. She glanced up from her bench and grinned. Two of her students followed suit with knowing glances. I must be so obvious.

"Yes, Professor," she said, her disarming smile spreading across her lips.

"Can I see you for a moment?"

She put her pen down and took off her gloves. Deliberately slow, so I stood there in the doorway on full display. No one takes off gloves so slowly. I grinned again like a teen, it practically leapt onto my face.

She came into the hallway and I held the door open for her — intending to keep it open so the students wouldn't think of it as a personal visit. She nodded, and I could tell she appreciated the gesture.

"I'm trying to find the daycare to check on the little girl, and I can't find the right door. Do you know where it is?"

She regarded me quizzically, and I saw tears welling up in her eyes. She drew a short breath and breathed slowly. Swinging her hip against the door, it closed slowly and left us alone in the hallway.

"What daycare?"

My eyes narrowed. I couldn't be sure if she was playing around with me, or if I'd said something offensive. Why did her emotions change so fast?

"The… daycare around the corner where the kids are? The one I found in the hallway?" I said trying to jog her memory.

"There's no daycare here. I've been in this building since the day it opened. I've never even seen kids."

"Not possible," I said incredulously, "I was there. I held her hand. I was coming back from dropping her off when you… saved me."

Her forehead furrowed with concern.

"I'm not saying there aren't kids in the building, but there is no daycare I know of."

She flushed red and quickly opened the door back up, pushing it all the way so it latched open.

The students glanced up and then quickly back down.

"Pam, I…" I choked out.

"It's okay," she said, smiling and wiping a tear.

"They were probably playing in the building. Or got the room for the afternoon. Who knows." I added trying to change the subject.

After a second, she smiled again, the sparkle in her eyes returning. Leaning forward she put her hand on my chest. So much for subtlety. I saw the same two students gaze back up directly at us. This time I gave them the "hey, what's a boy to do?" expression.

"I gotta get back to these guys before they blow something up." She said, loudly on purpose. All heads snapped back to their microscopes.

I silently nodded and smiled. Quickly I backed out of the door and she turned back in, grabbing another pair of gloves from the bench.

This can't be right.

Again, I turned back down the hallway to find the daycare, when I got to the door I turned the knob to walk in. Locked. I jiggled the handle and knocked. No response.

For a minute I stood staring at the door. Maybe there isn't a daycare. This could be a multipurpose room they were using for the day. It would explain her getting lost. I let my brain take that for truth. Still, something itched in my mind. How could Pamela have never seen kids when I see them all the time?

For the next two days, I couldn't keep my mind together. I thought about Saturday night constantly. Ice cream after work functioned as the "safe date." You didn't have many expectations and it lacked a sense of impending commitment. Dinner at her place came with different implications. Kind of fast in my book, but at my age, why waste the time?

In anticipation, I made sure I wore something new to her: My grey sport coat, black shirt, burgundy suspenders, tan trousers, and my burnt-brown wingtips. Dressy, but still casual, it's not a job interview or anything. Right?

We arranged for me to be there at 7:00, but I wouldn't knock until 7:05. I figured it would give her enough time to finish up if things were running behind, but not enough to drive her crazy with anticipation if she had been ready and waiting for me. My ex always ran behind, long-term training I needed to unlearn I suppose.

I swung by the grocery store on the way to Centre Hall to pick up some wine and roses. Riesling and Yuengling lager. This was central PA after all.

Then the debate… to buy the condoms or not? I stared at the box for a few minutes.

A college student came by and grabbed a box of twelve like buying a box of tissues.

Why is this not easier? This wasn't something married people even thought about, and I hadn't bought a box since the 90s.

I took a cue from the youngster, and I threw a three-pack into my basket and moved on.

The girl behind the counter smiled as I paid for my order.

"Have a fun time!" She intoned as I took up my parcel.

"Thanks, I will," I said, but I couldn't help translate in my head as "I hope you get lucky!"

At 6:50 I got to Pamela's neighborhood, a few blocks off the main drag. The diminutive town of Centre Hall possessed a singular Main Street and then everything branched off it. I'd gotten to her house quickly, a small white affair, simple, quaint. A nice garden and clothesline in the back; definitely hers. I pulled into the driveway of the two-car garage and parked right next to her car.

I arrived at 7:00 on the dot, immediately popped in a piece of gum, and chewed furiously. The sun shone fairly high in the sky, but I saw the porch lights come on and the drapes move slightly. My hand immediately started shaking. The exquisite panic you got in situations like this. Still, I found myself enjoying the rush.

I grabbed the roses and the alcohol mentally felt the "lucky pack" in my coat, swallowed the gum, and got out of the car. Glancing around the neighborhood I tried to look as casual as possible but felt all the eyes of her unseen neighbors boring into me. I saw no one, the street was deserted. Dead plants covered her neighbor's porch. No birds either. Just the sound of a lawnmower in the distance. I swallowed hard, cleared my throat, and stepped onto her porch.

I knocked, rapping out "Shave and a Haircut." I waited a moment, and then I heard the lock click and the door open.

Framed in the doorway and against the stairs, stood a vision of beauty. Her hair coiled up in a half bun, half loose; like she threw it together before she opened the door, but I knew the difference. She wore a simple green dress with spaghetti straps, it hugged her lines without revealing too much. Subtle brown eyeshadow, and rose-colored lipstick, barefoot with red painted nails; it took all my concentration to pull off my best Joe Cool.

"Hey, that is some dress." With that, I became the least articulate man on Earth.

She smiled. My knees wobbled. Again.

"This is literally the only clean thing I could find." She said. She had to be lying. "I'm glad you like it."

Doing the best cocktail gymnastics with my hands as I could, I held up the roses and the drinks.

"These go with German food, right? I mean you can't go wrong with beer."

Sigh. Smooth, Kevin.

"Thank you!" She said, taking the roses out of my hand. "They are beautiful."

She noticed my coat open — which I forgot to button — and scanned my outfit.

"Suspenders?" She said, raising her eyebrows.

"I hate belts," I said dismissively.

"I was never a suspenders girl, but you make them work."

I couldn't tell if she complimented me or not.

"Dinner smells amazing!" I said and meant it honestly.

She beamed and curtsied playfully.

After standing there for a few seconds, I gestured over to the kitchen for us to put down the items. She smiled and we turned in.

The kitchen was simple: wooden cabinets painted white, understated floral wallpaper. Functional with a hint of decoration.

"Nice place," I said as I opened up the fridge to chill the drinks.

"Thank you. It's small and quiet. I like it."

I set the drinks in an empty spot, then turned around, Pamela stood right behind me, vase in hand.

I smiled and unwrapped the roses, I knew they needed to be cut, but her eyes told me the water would be enough. I put them in quickly, being careful to pay attention and not hook myself on a thorn. It took all my concentration to put the vase on the table.

"I guess the roses worked huh?" I said, already knowing this music, like a forgotten song from my youth.

She put her hands into my coat, grabbed my suspenders, and pulled me in for a kiss.

"What about dinner?" I said breathlessly between kisses, not caring about the food.

"Dinner can wait."

With a surprising amount of strength, she pulled me out of the kitchen by my suspenders. I flashed a glance to the front door — she must have closed it behind me — and followed her up the stairs.

Hours later we came back down. The sun had set, June bugs and fireflies filled the air. A soft, cool breeze drifted through the kitchen windows. She wore my shirt, French cuffs rolled up and I wore my pants and undershirt, suspenders dropped.

"Let's eat, I'm starving," she said, hurriedly going to the crockpot and ladling out the sausage and potato soup she made.

I pulled out two chairs for us and went to the fridge to get the drinks, then I helped her set the table. A simple display, with the roses and two candles as the centerpiece. With such great company, it was more beautiful than any fancy restaurant I have been in. Everything felt right. Perfect.

"You're still hungry huh?" I asked with a roguish smile.

She rolled her eyes and kicked me under the table.

I feigned pain and mouthed an "ow."

After a few minutes, I sat staring at her over the top of my beer. Soft lines. Crooked wry smile. Hair tossed.

"What?" she asked, I could see her embarrassment.

I smiled, "Nothing, just looking at you. It's the only time in my life I am glad I took a shot in the face. I never saw this coming."

"I'm glad you have a glass jaw, Champ," she teased.

I smiled back, holding her gaze.

Another breeze blew in from the window, a little cooler than before. The breezes usually blew down from the mountains at night. It will be a welcome relief in August, but in June it can still be chilly. I motioned to the window; silently asking if she wanted me to close it. She pulled down the sleeves of my shirt and nodded.

I grabbed the sash and started pulling the window down; children were playing across the street.

"Why am I always seeing kids?" I asked her, as I stared out at the small forms silhouetted against the moonlight. "Why are they out this late?"

Pamela gazed up from her wine and paused a few moments before speaking, suddenly distant.

"Do you see these kids?" I asked for confirmation.

"They are free-range in this neighborhood. It feels safe here. It's why I moved in."

I came back over to the table and sat down.

"I never asked, do you have kids? Obviously, there aren't any here." I said.

Pamela got quiet. Damn. It made sense.

"I'm sorry sweetheart, I didn't put two and two together."

She smiled weakly, not a happy one, but one inured to the pain.

"You're one of the most brilliant people I know, but slow on the uptake sometimes."

I nodded silently, then added, "But I'm pretty."

Another eye-roll, this time with a snort of a laugh. She shook her head again and took a deep breath.

"I did. She died ten years ago. Leukemia."

"My God, I'm so sorry." I reached across the table and took her hand.

"Thanks." She sighed. "After she... died, my marriage kinda died with it. So, I went back to school. Got my masters and doctorate at Iowa State, then came here for post-doc."

"Oncology. You're trying to find a cure."

"Of course, wouldn't you?" tears started welling up in her eyes.

"Hey, you don't have to talk about it. I didn't mean to upset you."

She tried to smile through her tears. "It's Okay. I trust you. I have a feeling you aren't going to freak out on me and run like the others."

She was right.

"Hang on, I'll get you a picture." She went back upstairs, and I started cleaning up in the kitchen — as best as I could without knowing things like the location of dishes. I could still see the kids in the streetlight, but now in front of the house. Again, they were in costume.

I raised an eyebrow.

"Okay, this isn't a special event. What the hell is going on?"

Pamela came back down, picture frame in hand. I'd seen it in the bedroom, but it had been too dark to make out the photo at the time.

"This is my baby," she said with pride, mixed with longing and sadness.

I looked at the photo; a little girl about five. Walnut brown hair. Startling olivine eyes.

"Darlene," we said at the same time.

Gleeful giggling and hurried whispers came from the front porch, then the sound of children playing.

We both heard it.

THANK YOU FOR READING!

I hope you enjoyed reading this anthology. It was created over the long haul of the coronavirus pandemic of 2020-2021. Some people made sourdough bread; I wrote science fiction.

If you liked the anthology, please leave a review on my Amazon page: https://www.amazon.com/SG-Kubrak/e/B08BJH7DSS?ref_=dbs_p_ebk_r00_abau_000000

Follow me on Twitter: @sgkubrak

Visit my author page: www.sgkubrak.com

Keep reading for an excerpt of "Jessica Unbound" the debut novel, Now Available on Kindle, and Print!

Excerpt from "Jessica Unbound"

The hulking alien stared down at Jessica's small frame and smiled. The translucent amber square floating above its wrist spoke.

"You understand me now, Terran?" it said in perfect English.

"I do!" Jessica beamed. "You learned English when I was learning… Standard?" She paused to search her memory for the proper word to describe their language.

"Obviously. We could have stayed with Latin, though. I find it much more descriptive. Germanic languages are so harsh, like my friend here."

Hand quickly to her face, Jessica tried to suppress a giggle. She glanced at the dark green eyes of the alien, but it did not respond.

"It doesn't speak it yet?"

"My companion, Orvalus, does not yet know how to speak English. He will step into The Teacher and learn as you did."

The square switched to Standard and spoke briefly to the tall alien.

At the hearing of his name, Orvalus stood more erect and placed his hand over the center of his chest, bowing slightly. Jessica responded and respectfully stepped back.

In a quick two strides, Orvalus cleared the span of the room and stepped into the leftmost arch. With the calm of someone who had been through the process hundreds of times, he grabbed the helmet and snapped it onto his head. In a second his eyes closed and his body twitched gently.

"How…?" Jessica asked.

"Brainwave manipulation."

The voice of the square permeated the room, coming from everywhere and nowhere.

"The Teacher manipulates the brainwaves of the student and in so doing, alters its structure and neurotransmitters. Your Terran brain is more primitive and transference is more difficult and time consuming. However, it afforded the ability to learn many things about you."

Jessica felt a slight twinge of offense as Orvalus stepped back out of the arch, releasing the helmet to hang in the space.

"Hello, Jessica," he said when he stepped out and spoke in a deep, resonant baritone. "I can understand you now. We can speak both languages now. There should be… no lapse in communication."

"I'm the only version of English you have here? What about all the Latin and Cantonese?" She spoke into the air, hoping the square would respond.

It did, this time from Orvalus's wrist.

"The gate to Terra has not been open in some time. We have not had any visitors from your dimension since the Time of the Trials. None of them spoke English."

"How long ago? Wait… dimension? So, I am in another dimension?"

"That is correct, Terran. You are in another reality to your own. The portal network can traverse spacetime as well as different dimensions. Parallel existences, to put it in a phrase your culture can understand."

Jessica accepted the fact quickly. So easily she surprised herself. If this were in fact a delusion, she was obliged to follow it to its conclusion. If this were real, then the same properties of wormholes in spacetime could conceivably apply to other dimensions. She moved on quickly from the mental gymnastics and focused on the matter at hand.

The square switched back to the room.

"It has been one hundred fifty-seven standard years since the last Terran visit. Eighteen-hundred years on Terra."

Ever the student of history and centers of learning, she deftly reached a conclusion. "The gate was in Rome?"

Orvalus stepped back, surprised. The square waited a moment before speaking. "Very perceptive. You surprise me, Terran."

"The gates link into a multiverse, with time and space as variables?"

Orvalus chuckled as he walked into the main room with the frame. "You know much small one. Careful Dee, she is… smarter than you think."

ABOUT THE AUTHOR

S.G. Kubrak has been writing — starting with the ridiculously sized "so big" crayons — on any surface he could since before he could walk, much to the family's chagrin.

S.G. spends a great deal of time trying to explain quantum entanglement, and how it relates to the "hero's journey" without the use of pictures or dense mathematics. A lover of gardening and working with his hands, he is often compared to Pa Ingalls, without the fiddle. His proudest accomplishment is teaching his daughter the essence of good pizza and bagels.

He lives with his wife and daughter in suburban Virginia, but his heart is always in his native New Jersey.

He is currently writing the sequel to his first novel *Jessica Unbound*, *Jessica Unbound: Gaia*.

Made in the USA
Las Vegas, NV
21 May 2024

90199745R00100